Illusions
Of
a
Love Story

To Kim

May the journey
be everything
you hoped for!
Keep up the good
work
Nadia Aidan

Illusions
Of
a
Love Story

The love that stood strong for one,
showed the love was eternally true...

Intertwining Two Views Of Love To Find One.

Nadia Aidan

iUniverse, Inc.
New York   Bloomington

Illusions of a Love Story

Cover art put together, Jane Duncan
Facilitator Of Creations
http://janeduncan.com

With thanks to NASA, ESA, and the Hubble Heritage Team
(STScI/AURA) ESA/Hubble Collaboration for use of Barred Spiral Galaxy NGC 1672

iUniverse books may be ordered through booksellers or by contacting:

iUniverse
1663 Liberty Drive
Bloomington, IN 47403
www.iuniverse.com
1-800-Authors (1-800-288-4677)

ISBN: 978-0-595-52541-6 (pbk)
ISBN: 978-0-595-62594-9 (ebk)

Printed in the United States of America

iUniverse rev. date: 10/23/08

Contents

❀

Foreword

❀

The best way to read this is to let the words resonate with the heart. Where the mind cannot follow, the heart will understand. When we do not listen to the mind, the space to hear the heart grows wider. These words exist beneath the mind.

Thomas Whitmire

Foreword
⚜

This is pure. No one outside of the love has looked at this until now. I invite you to read this in a certain way. Programmed world, this is different.

Look for the pattern. What speaks to you?

What are your lessons?

This comes from her hands and heart directly to you, untouched with pure love.

In all its imperfections it is just like life.

Please let the little imperfections remind you about the mysteries of life. Embrace those imperfections as you do that with life, then you can let yourself be imperfect.

In this programmed world imperfection is not always viewed as right, what do you think that mindset does to your view of yourself and others?

In your hand is this bundle of love...it is straight from the heart...it is pure and has not been touched by any nonbelievers...

This is a very special and unique book as it comes to you with so much love to give. Be open to it. Notice the conversation in your heart as you read this. Is your mind wrestling with the program of this not following the correct format or grammar? Or are you engrossed in the beauty and mystery of life so much that the imperfections add to the uniqueness of the experience?

I hope this story in some way helps you to see different views of life and the mystery each of us have when we open our hearts and minds. Remember to be open. Stay open…When you find that you are not open, because there will be a time you aren't, then all you have to do is just observe and notice… then you are open again.

Terri Coleman

A Loving Note

❀

This is very personal to me. It is my journey and now I am sharing it with you. Until now, my only way to share was when meeting people in person.

This story only touches on a few of my experiences and much was left out relating to the love of all that has happened to me. This book was only edited and viewed from a few that know the story and have shared some of the experiences with me. I trusted my guidance to show me a new way to write about these experiences. This book is formatted differently, so allow yourself with patience and understanding to grasp what you can.

Even though the intellect may not be able to understand everything as you read this book, trust that your soul will. Some of the information is channeled, and comes in directly from the spirit guides. The channeled words are *italicized*. So when I channel, I relive and write these experiences freely without the worry of proper grammar and punctuation as you the reader would normal expect.

I feel like there are parts of the story that go on and on, but in a way that is how my life was during my transformation.

The story does jump, at times you will find yourself reading one thing, then the story line jumps to another. As you know, life jumps from one thing to the next, and my story begins.

Introduction

❀

"So many illusions of meaning reside in this book."
  Life is a reality: It is the illusion of what we believe to be real.
Yet, does it take just one to come to the strength and hope to help others. To
let the eyes be open to one illusion, one small belief of what they cannot see
to be real. This reality is the base and all elements, to make what you feel
in your heart to be real. It does take the strength of only one to believe. It
holds such an existence to create all that you wish to create. -- Channeled
from the elders.

Perhaps we should start with the meaning of channeled thru the
elders. The experiences shared thru out this book came to me as I
agreed to be still and listen with belief and clarity to those I call the
elders. The easiest way to explain this is, I actual see a spirit speaking
directly to my spirit. And then the information comes through. And
when this happens, words and terms are used to the best of my ability
to get the message across.

When I write my soul is understanding the message received
through the spirit. This information is then processed through my
physical form and it appears on the page in a new way.

Can one explain the depths of this illusion, the illusion I felt in my
heart to be so real. The depths of holding hope to come to a place to
touch other lives. Can it make a difference with all the pain that has

given, to come to this place to trust. Trust into existence something that is not seen, something that is hidden. To find a true place that lies within the heart, a place that only one can find within them. This place is something that you can find. This place starts with accepting one belief, in one thing - you.

It does not matter that the illusion created is a stronger belief in love. It does not hold only one hope for myself, but hope for others. Others in which you can foresee to bring hope. If one begins, then the others will find a place to begin for themselves. It takes small steps to honor, and small steps to proceed.

I have voiced much of my story and that story comes from the heart. Does it matter if the heart of one tried to make a difference? Does that one begin to believe in hope? I held so much pain for the ones I lost, and for the ones I have given up. The pain lingered as each step brought me to a journey into the light. Each step showed my own strengths, and each step took me further in following my heart; a heart that has touched hundreds already. A story to be told that will reach out to bring light into ones eyes. Was it all worth it? I guess I would have to say it was. It effected so many, and yet, I still hold hope that those will be brought back to me. It was time this illusion was brought forward to make a difference. This is the illusion I created to bring about that change. To let one foresee it, begins by taking a stand, to have some small hope that you can make it happen. Do I honor all that was hidden in the shadows for me? I guess I can say I do. For those hidden shadows were the answers that unlocked a sacred place. A key that we all have been looking for - that key is the key you hold. That key is given by others to help and heal, and lead you on the way. The trust of others is the trust you have honored for yourself.

Do I truly believe, the love that I have for the one made a difference in me? Yes. That love helped me find the love within myself.

I was given the strength by surrendering to all, and sacrificing much of what we like to call reality. For this, I have given myself the strength to move on and to help and to heal and to trust that it will make a difference. I trusted in the guidance,; I trusted in the unknown. Some times we don't believe what we cannot see and therefore are blinded to see the forwards we should take. If I can be the one that shows some hope, some proof then my journey was well worth it.

I embraced so many blessings, I embraced so many hopes, and I embraced and touched the one true thing we all yearn for.

I touched, LOVE.

The illusion is the hidden secret of things. Things we have stored in our hearts to be triggered and opened to help us remember…

My words fall into the veers of existence
I write with compassion
I feel all sanctuary of love
A mere lavish of words
To the depths of veils thru the vast existence of the unknown
Thru to mere peaks of a world that is in itself unknown
To bring to existence flowering of softness spoken to carry itself
thru the faints of the stillness the Universe holds
I reside there yet live here
Why must we suffer in this world
Where all existence holds a placement of survival and confusion
To find the one true thing each one is searching
A true meaning that has not left its way of voicing for centuries
To repeat itself over ....
Then it seems you both have to arrive first... Arriving in each
other

Chapter I

OVER AND OVER

She walks out of the back door and the trees overcome her with all the beauty they hold. She places her body in a chair on the deck, and swirls it around as it rustles the wood underneath her feet. Placing it in the same spot she does each night, to face the view between the trees and watch the evening sky. The air is warm, as the night gives a soft feeling to the breeze. She leans back, with her legs up and escapes into the moonlit night.

After a few hours she stands, raising her arms, wanting to grab just one more glitter in the sky. She always feels the connection to the moon and the shimmer of each bright star. Each night she repeats herself, going beyond shadows, to simple gaze into the stillness. The connection with the night sky has been strong these last few years. For a few moments her mind is free, escaping all that she has endeavored.

Walking back through the door, she goes into the bathroom. Looking into the mirror, she sees an image of years. Being in her mid-thirties, she wonders where all the years have gone. The grey has become through her blonde hair, and darkness has fallen under her eyes.

She stares straight ahead voicing, "Hope" the name that was given to her all those years back.

Stating to herself, "How can I be with such a strong name, yet have no hope for myself?"

She takes herself and lays on the couch, turning the television on to escape once again into whatever she can. Thinking, it has been over two years now that he has been gone. The man she loved, her best friend, a man she spent eleven years with. Even until this day, she holds such unconditional love for him. She lets her thoughts go back into the television, and not let that come into her mind.

The next day, she awakes going back to the every day-to-day life. This is the life that seems to repeat itself over and over - same routine, same job, same everything. As she looks into the mirror, she realizes the "she" has turned into "I."

~I, "Hope," a figment of who I am. ~

It brings all of me to form a story of hardship over these last few years. Wondering, I really have let all my life go. I was ready to acknowledge what I have taken on for myself.

I then took my body over to the couch and fell into a deep trance of all that has come. Letting it all begin from this day forward.

I decided at that moment to take a day off. I called into work and told them I needed a few days to process some more things. I went downstairs and put on a pot of coffee. I grabbed the phone to call my friend Sam, short for Samantha. She was an old friend from back home. Waiting to dial, I went into thought -- a daydream state.

I don't have any friends here - they fall into the realm of being all far in between. I was not finding it easy to be so alone since moving here. My husband was transferred quite a few years back, so we left our home state. The move seems to have shifted my life in all directions and changed it in so many ways.

Suddenly, I remembered my neighbor, Darleen, whom I seemed to be forming a friendship with. I had begun to know her fairly well and talk with her on occasion. She is older than I am, but our conversations seem to have some connectedness of understanding. She is very open to what was happening to me and going over to chat felt comforting. I have tried to stop analyzing the unknown of what has taken over my life. Sitting, talking and having coffee was nice sometimes. This new friendship had become a place to release all these things, and a place I felt support. I have come to a state of not analyzing the unknown - of not analyzing what I felt was taking over my life. I had come from being a "normal" person with a "normal" nine-to-five job, and now I wasn't even sure what was real anymore.

Oh yeah, I was going to call Sam. I grabbed a cup and filled it up with coffee, and dialed Sam. She answered and as we talked she said I should consider moving back. My insides started to feel frustration, and in a louder tone I told her, "No, I can't explain what is happening to me. I don't feel that moving back is the right choice. Can we let this be the last time we bring that up?" I can always hear the worry in her voice when I speak to her. "Sam, I think I am going to quit my job!" In the short silence that followed, I voiced to her,

"What else can I do?"

"I have decided I am coming for a visit," she said after a pause. Then she stated, "I am going to stay for a few weeks."

"That sounds great, the sooner the better!"

"Good," with excitement in her voice, "I will book the flight today."

"So, I guess it is settled and I will see you as soon as you get here." I was relieved that Sam was coming; I could use her support right now.

I grabbed my cup of coffee and headed out on the deck. Darlene was walking out of the house, and waved hello. I turned towards her, raised my mug,

"Hello, neighbor."

"Come over, lets talk," she said.

I crossed the yard and went inside, walking through the house, and into the sun room. We sat quietly and she stared at me. She knew about the strange things that had been happening to me.

"Hope, you know we can talk about this," she said looking compassionately at me.

I wasn't even sure where to begin, without sounding crazy. Grabbing my hands and holding them up to my face, I started to cry.

Her husband came in and we all started to talk. He quietly sat and observed the conversation. I voiced to both of them what I was going through. I told them how I had been having strange experiences and how I knew things were going to happen before they actually did.

~ How I have always seen things at night -- shadows in the night. ~

I told them about my earlier years, all about my childhood.

"Ever since I was a small girl, I would wake up and see a person in my room. A transparent see-through looking shadow, but looking like a person. The shadow would remain holding every detail of an actual person. When I got older it happened more and more. This occurred a lot when I was in college. My friends and I looked up sleep disorders, night terrors, everything. I would never admit it was a spirit standing next to my bed. This phenomenon seems to have re-emerged, and it is happening all the time now. The spirit's appearances are becoming more pronounced, making it difficult for me to sleep. I have been staying up all night, keeping the TV on so I don't fall asleep. It is so vivid, and when I do fall asleep they seem to wake me up. I feel like something is tugging or tapping on me."

Once I started talking I couldn't stop, so I went on, "Other things are happening and occurring. I was on the phone the other day with a friend and I saw an event happen. I could see her standing in the kitchen talking with her boyfriend. I was seeing exactly what they were talking about and their placement in a kitchen. I told my friend what I was seeing. She called me back a few days later, and recounted the event exactly as I saw it - even the words of their conversation."

They both stared at me, and then said, "We believe you and we believe in all of this. If you ever need to talk, we will listen."

I wanted to tell them more. It felt good to be able to trust someone. I wanted to tell them more about the past year, my drinking, and all the other unexplainable events. Mainly, I wanted to tell them about my latest experience, but I thought it was not the right time. This was already hard enough for me to admit so I thanked them for the coffee as I left.

"Please come back tomorrow," Darleen said.

I went back home to sleep for the rest of the day. When I sleep during the day nothing odd seems to happen; that was, no transparent shadows emerged in the lightness of the day. When I woke up, I grabbed the phone to call Sam. We often stayed on the phone for hours.

As I was talking to her, I started to feel very strange. I went into the bathroom and noticed my eyes looked dilated. For some unknown reason, I told her to ask me any question. I felt like I had answers. Yes and No's would keep flowing out of my mouth in response to her questions. We were both surprised and she asked, "What was that?"

"I don't know, Sam," is the only answer I could give.

"Hope, your answers to each question seems to be right on. I asked you questions about some events that have happened. One question was about my friend, Beth, getting a job that she wanted. The Yes and No's for each question matched."

"I can't explain it, Sam. It is so weird. I am starting to feel dizzy, I think I should go. I will talk to you soon."

I did my normal routine each day, except I seemed to have lost my appetite for eating. I would just clean the house and keep busy. When I was cleaning the house one day, I felt I should go to the library.

I headed to the local library, walking in the air was filled with a strong musty smell. I was searching for a book; someone had given me once, about a man who sees spirits. I found the book and others that were related to psychics or mediums. I checked each book out, and then headed home.

I got home and placed the books on my nightstand next to the bed. I put on my pajamas and laid in bed, picking up the first book. As I started to read it, I felt uneasy and very strange, and then I heard, '*Put it down.*'

It freaked me out and I threw the book down. I started to voice out loud to myself, "Okay, breathe and pick the book up." I picked up a different one, and the same thing happened. I threw that book down, too, and stared at the walls.

~ I have sensed things in my mind, but this was actually the first encounter with the voice so loud in my head. ~

I stayed up all night, watching television; finally, early in the morning I went to Darleen's. I knew she could tell I hadn't slept, so I told her how I was unable to read any of the books that I checked out from the library.

"I am not kidding you; it was literally a loud and clear voice in my head telling me to put the book down."

We sat and talked for awhile, but I still felt so much despair. "I feel like my life has flashed before my eyes and nothing seems normal anymore," I said as I looked at Darleen. Then I went on to say, "What is normal? Are we here to just be here? Should I sit in this state of mind, analyzing this day in and day out?"

My mind seemed to be racing a mile a minute. Then it stopped for a split second and I could hear a bird outside and see the sun beaming through the screen.

"Hope, maybe it will all make sense in due time... try to let it be."

"My friend Sam is coming in a few days. She got a flight after I spoke with her. Sam and I became good friends right before I left my hometown of St. Louis.

When all this started, she would listen and listen for hours. She always has a calmness to her and would speak to me in a soft tone - never judging what I had to say, only listening.

She knows the nights were and still can be sleepless and hard. When I cannot sleep, she stays on the phone with me. Even though Sam and I cannot explain all of this, she tries to talk me through what I am seeing. We have a strong bond of friendship. Something seems to be connecting us deeper - especially with all this happening."

"She sounds like a great friend to have. I am glad she is coming," Darleen expressed.

"Yeah, one time, I had a vision and saw our arms criss-crossed over each others, holding onto one another's forearms. Then I watched in the vision as a bright white rope wrapped around and through our arms. I sensed it was a sign of protection."

"I guess I should go now," I said as I looked and saw the sun was going down.

As I walked in the back door, I could hear the silence. My eyes glanced around the large living area, furniture so neatly in its place. This house was quite big and the space seemed so surreal for one person. I put some hot water on, and then waited to go sit in my normal spot under the stars. Things seemed to be coming to me, thoughts and so many understatements. I grabbed a notebook and thought, why not write? Maybe, writing the words down on paper would do some good.

Notebook in one hand, warm tea in the other, I stepped out onto the deck and pulled a table close to my chair to set my stuff upon. I stared down at the pen and blank piece of paper. Then I heard something in my mind say, '*Time to start writing.*'

There are those voices again, the ones I couldn't make sense of... since they began.

Suddenly, words started flowing through my mind. I grabbed my pen, touched the paper and began to write.

I sat, writing the endeavors that have taken so much of my mind - my feelings, and my thoughts of all that has occurred. When I finished, I realized the tea was cold and the breeze had given a chill to the air. I walked inside to get comfortable. I sank into the couch feeling very light headed. I looked down at the notebook that was still in my hand.

I really didn't even remember writing much. The time seem to go by so fast, yet I had written so many pages. When I looked, most of it seemed to be more poetic than any events that have occurred. I realized exactly that, pages filled with poems, poetic lines, one after another. I flipped through and found one that caught my eye. I sat back on the couch and began to read it out loud:

> *The night has such tightness in the air*
> *The chimes bring a song from each lair*
> *She stands freely with the moon glimmering...*
> *all the stories for them to hear*
> *Breathing the coldness and feeling some despair*
> *His love dances to the songs of the wind that she*
> *only bares*

Interesting, I thought. This sounds like a love poem. Then something else jumped out at me. I remember writing this and wondered after I wrote it what it truly meant:

> '*The last and final one would be an unknown, just by having a conversation with him would change the person you used to be; to the person you needed to be.*'

Interesting again, yet this was very different. I closed the notebook and was feeling tired. I walked up the stairs and turned the television on, changed, washed my face and then crawled into bed.

Once again it happened; I was startled in the middle of the night and had to rub my eyes because standing next to my bed was a shadow of a woman. I could see her clear as day - her dark wavy hair, the white blouse and even her facial features. I quickly grabbed the covers and pulled them over my head. I slowly pulled the covers down and in a flash she was right in my face. I could feel my heart racing and I just wanted to cry. I screamed, "Go away, please leave me alone!"

This brought back to me all those horrible memories. It had been a long time since I had been this scared. She got so close and this was the closest ever. I remembered my husband used to stay up with me until I fell asleep. I would get so scared and wake up sweating and shaking. He would always tell me I was fine, and then would even joke about it the next day. Laughing and saying, "Do you remember talking to all your ghostly buddies last night?"

As I rolled into those thoughts, I fell asleep. The night shifted into a new day. As I sat up, I thought about my writings. What did it mean, 'the last and final one' and who was I going to change into?

I got ready and drove into the office to talk to my boss. I walked through the revolving door and down the hallway to her office. She waved her hand for me to take a seat, while she finished her call. I voiced to her I wasn't going to be working anymore, that I would not be back.

"I felt that for awhile, Hope," she said, not looking surprised. She paused for a brief moment, and with compassion in her voice said, "I have already made arrangements for someone to replace you. Don't worry about putting your two weeks in. It will be handled. Take the time you need."

I thanked her and said, "Good-bye."

What a relief. I felt I had made the right decision. The office seemed so quiet as everyone continued working at their desks.

I had sweat pants on, an old t-shirt and running shoes. I felt that I should go back to the lake and start running again. I was feeling to go running there for awhile and kept sensing it had something to do with the trees.

When I arrived, I parked my jeep in the corner and went up the stairs. The stairs led to a paved path all covered with trees. It had rained some the night before and the pavement was still wet. I walked at first taking my time and looking at the trees. I never noticed how amazing the barks of trees were after it rained. They were saturated with wetness which made them seem to come alive. Each step I took, I admired the liveliness the trees held.

I began to run and ran all the way around the lake with my eyes focused on the pavement. I did not want to look up in fear that someone may see me crying.

After I was done running, I felt alive. I sat in my jeep and looked for something to write on. I reached my hand under the seat and grabbed something. It was a notebook hidden under my seat. I looked at it, remembering this notebook. I had written in it many months prior but had never read it. I vaguely remember writing in it, because of my intoxicating state from the effects of alcohol.

I found a blank page and started to write. The thoughts flowed and the words seemed to capture each moment precisely on the page.

This time, I wrote all about the men that I had encountered in the last year. These, to me, were not any ordinary men; they were men that I needed to mend my heart with. I know this because, after a period of ten months all knowledge was given to me with much understanding. It all became clear with that phase of men, once the cycle of ten months was up.

All the past life karma that needed to be fixed was mended. I met each man, dealt with physically being in their presence, and mended all that was in the past.

I sat thinking and then decided to take the reading of this further when Sam got into town. She was coming tomorrow morning, and I wanted to get her response on all of it. She always brought so much light to all the encounters with the men. It seems to all relate with the phenomena of my karma connections. I was about to flip the notebook closed, when I saw at the end a page titled.

'Past lives, mending of lives left, to mend the heart.'

That title really made so much sense to me now. What I sensed with this was:

I went to the past to remember, to bring that experience to the now. This mends the karma that I had from before. By mending this in the now, it has mended my heart.

I drove home to clean and get ready for Sam. I pulled into the long narrow driveway stopping halfway and I stared at the large brick two story house. The yard landscaped with beauty, which I spent hours to obtain. The picture perfect salt box brick house that I had always wanted. I pulled into the garage and walked past some memories that lay in the corner.

I cleaned the rest of the day until evening. Then I took my lethargic body to sit on the deck and stare out into the night. The clouds were hazy and the night eerie. The air felt thick, and for some reason it did not seem right outside, so I decided to go to bed early.

I woke with a startle, sitting upright and staring into the hallway. A figure appeared an image of the same woman I had seen the night before. I ran to the door and slammed it shut. It took me awhile to fall back asleep only to wake up again. This time the figure came right through the door, and close up to my face. I was so scared I grabbed all the pillows and escaped into the depths of my bed. I eventually, fell asleep with the comfort of hiding within the covers that surrounded me.

I awoke with the alarm blaring in my ear. I jumped up and ran into the closet, threw my jeans on and raced outside. I had to pick Sam up from the airport and I was running late. I stood waiting with about thirty other people, and then I saw her. Our eyes met and I could feel through the excitement my stomach twisting.

"It is such a relief to see your face." I said.

"Hope, you look terrible! Your eyes are sunken in," she said with a worried look on her face.

"Thanks Sam, good to see you, too."

Then we both laughed and sighed as we stood embracing with a long hug.

As your mind sits quietly
An image, a split second when someone comes into mind
Then a smile that is a moment
You take the moment,
Then as the spilt second comes it is gone
Send it on its way with love
Then the silence begins again
The mind is a precious thing
One can enjoy a split moment
But what is truly a magical moment
is the silence
The silence of being here right now
in the moment
Then your eyes will only see in that moment

Chapter II

THE COMFORT

*T*he smile on her face seemed to put such easement to my mind. We gave each other another hug and I could feel the length of years that stood between us. We went to eat and then went straight to the house. This was the first time Sam had been to my house. She walked in the back door with me and stopped.

"Hope, I can feel the sorrow here," she said as she looked at me. "It feels sad, and the air feels heavy."

"Yeah Sam, the energy is intense."

"Energy?" she voiced, looking puzzled. "What are you talking about?"

"I have no idea Sam, what I even just said. I had never even used the word energy."

We went into the living room and I lit a fire.

"I made us some coffee. You already know about the drinking. You know that story about my over consumption of alcohol and how it is no longer on my list of consuming."

I drank so much in the last year to forget about the pain. Then one day, I no longer felt the desire to drink anymore. I spoke with her at length about this change - no longer needing the alcohol to survive.

"Hope, maybe the alcohol shut this off in a way."

It was true; this was not the first time this had happened. The drinking began when the men came into my life. The visions were happening so often and so quickly at that time. I was seeing so many things.

When I started drinking the unexplainable became quieter. I was able to go to the bar and drink without telling anyone anything. I would get lost, night after night within the darkness of the bar.

"Now everything is back. Sam, you know what that means."

"Maybe, you should not hide from this anymore."

She knew that when I was hearing voicing in my mind, the only way to make it stop was the alcohol.

Each night I could drink enough to come home and pass out. I would pass out, wake up, drink a pot of coffee then start drinking again after work.

Back then I did not even process the voices. I ignored it, now I was finally admitting to it. The more I admit to it, the stronger it would come in. It did not start getting adamant and loud until I bought the books and the voice said, '*Put it down.*'

"Now, tell me about these writings," she said as she turned her head smiling.

"Well, the poems are nice and they are actually quite beautiful," voicing this and thinking to myself how surprised even I am about their beauty.

"Can you read me some of them?"

I got the notebook out, and read the first one from the other night, then this one:

> *Open your hands put your arms out*
> *Close your eyes*
> *What do you see*
> *What do you feel*
> *Open your heart*
> *Your heart will tell you*

"Maybe, the poems are helping me stay focused. I also found a notebook hidden under my seat." I was about to go get it from my jeep and stood up. All of sudden, I looked up at Sam and saw something next to her. I must have turned white as a ghost because Sam's face was shocked and her eyes remained stuck on me.

"Oh my gosh," I said, "Sam, I see a woman next to you. It is the same woman I have been seeing in the hallway." My mouth dropped, and I did not know if I should run or cry. I sat back down completely dazed.

"What does she look like, Hope?"

"Sam, I can see her clear as day," I said and then I described her. "She is an older woman, and she is holding up an apron -- waving the apron in front of her and moving it a certain way. I demonstrated the motion to her with my hands and body.

"It has to be my Nana, Hope. My Nana took her apron everywhere with her and use to do that same motion of a dance you just did. Can you hear her, what is she saying?"

"No, Sam how do I know what she is saying?"

Right after I said that, I could faintly hear a different voice in my mind. Sam and I could not make much sense of what was actually happening. Honestly, at this point neither of us cared; we just wanted to understand what I was seeing. Sam was not scared at all and only wanted to know what message her Nana was trying to get through.

"Sam, she is doing charades with me but I understand her."

I began telling Sam what her Nana was communicating to me, when the whole living room filled up with spirits. Freaking out I yelled at Sam,

"My whole living room is filling with spirits! Oh my gosh, Sam. What is happening?"

I took both of my hands and cupped them on the side of my face. I started to let the flow of harsh words come right out of my mouth.

"This is freaking me out!"

I kept my focus only on looking at her Nana, and relating to Sam what I could with the message. Sam seemed to respond as I voiced what I was getting.

"Hope, I never told you any of that."

"She is telling me that she visited you a few weeks ago."

Then her Nana described to me what she saw and heard at Sam's house. Sam's mouth now was dropping.

As I cupped my hand to get a view of her Nana, an older man kept popping in front of me. He was persistent, and would follow in front of my view as I moved my head. "Sam, there is an older man that will not stop popping in front of me."

"Does he look familiar?"

I let my focus zoom clear on the older man. "I can't believe this Sam, it is Lori's grandfather."

"No way, Hope. Can you hear him too?"

"Wait; hold on, this is too much." I took my focus back on Sam's Nana and she stop the charades and I was not hearing anything. "Sam she has stopped."

Sam started to say something, and I put my hand up to motion wait. I heard a faint, 'I love you, my little Sami.' Then I observed her Nana as she started to float backwards and faded away. Then the entire room emptied.

"What was that and how is this even possible!?!" Shouting as I jumped up quickly. With all that happened I thought I was going to faint.

"It was weird when I watched them leave, they all drifted backwards. Sam, they never turned their backs to me."

We talked for hours after this, replaying over and over what had happened. We talked about our friend Lori and her grandfather's death. Lori was another friend of mine from back home. All through school Sam, Lori and I were inseparable.

"Hope, are you going to call Lori?"

"I'm not sure yet, I still need to process all this first, let me sleep on it."

We decided to go to bed and do some thinking tomorrow. That night I actually slept and I could not believe it.

I woke up and made coffee while Sam was still asleep down the hall. I wrapped my robe around me and waited for the coffee, then went onto the deck. The sun had already filled the air with warmth. It was going to be a beautiful day. I grabbed my paper and wrote some more. The sun felt so energizing that it filled me with such a light of reassurance. It was as if I was hidden with only the rays of light surrounding me. As I wrote, I noticed that 'You' would start to jump into my sentences.

'You will be fine, hold your head high.'

"Am I writing to myself, am I writing to keep my strength?" Sam rolled out onto the deck with coffee in hand.

"Now I think it is time to release all of this," she said.

"Fine," I told her, "but I am not going back too many years. Maybe, just when all the strangeness of men came into my life."

"WAIT, let me grab a pillow," she laughed, saying, "I must get comfortable."

So it began the recapping of the last year. There were four men that came into my life with four different stories to share and four different horrors of obsession.

I suddenly realized as I took myself back into those memories, I found they all had a meaningful time line. They all came into my life for only one month, then a month in between. Except the first one, he was around for two months. We started with him and I wondered if it had anything to do with a visual that came into my mind. The visual had come while I was in his presence. I remember it clearly; it was odd and I had never shared it with anyone.

I was sitting in front of this desk of five people. In the vision when I looked to my left, the man I was attracted to was sitting right next to me. He was dressed in strange clothes -- not the kind of clothes you see everyday here. The five people spoke, and I told them that I wanted to be with him. They talked amongst themselves, and then pounded something like a gavel on the desk. It was like I was attending court in an alternate Universe. They said, "So be it" and something else that I did not understand, and then they vanished. Then the visual vanished and I never really understood it.

I was never physically intimate with this man, but I found myself thinking about him all the time.

We would run into each other at the bar while I was in my drinking phase and talk for hours. He was kind and somewhat flirtatious, but we never took it any further than that. I remember, whenever I would see him he would always try and look deep into my eyes. I remember telling him to stop looking at me like that. This made me feel strange, but yet I felt such a comfort being around him. He was in my life persistently for two months. Then one day, nothing, I felt nothing for him. I remember thinking how is this possible? I even went up to the bar that night, to test my feelings. When I saw him it was like I had never known or seen him before. It felt as if I had some type of amnesia. Nothing, I felt absolutely nothing. It was strange to feel this nothingness for him, but also a relief to have the thoughts about him leave my mind.

The way I met these men seemed irrelevant, the main focus was what happened to me. The obsession for each one was uncanny, and yet the experiences put such deep hurt in my heart. Each one came in for only a brief moment of time. Not one single one did I even go on a date with. Though, when I was talking to each one at the time, I was obsessed with each of them. It was to the point that when he did call, I would hang up the phone and sit by it - waiting and wondering when was he going to call again. Meanwhile, thinking each time I met these men, maybe they were the one.

One was an attraction so strong I could escape into his presence. That was the first one.

Another one, I shared intimacy with and that was filled with tearful nights. We were only together because of the alcohol and this always brought me to leave with him. I remember late one evening standing on his deck and staring into the sky crying. Saying to myself, please why, who is he, and where is he? I remembered the feeling so clearly it made my whole body tremble. I would stand there with that moment thinking where is he? Where is the one, will I find him?

The last two men I encountered were surrounded with negativity. Yet, I had the same lust of love with them as I did the others, along with the same obsession, and did not know why. The last two were the hardest to let go of and much was taken from my pride. Sam knew of them all because of the stories shared at night, when we were on the phone for hours. I refused to let the words even come out of my mouth with those last two. All the while during these difficult months I found myself voicing - "I need to find the one." I remember that clearly, "The one is he the one?"

I was not new to all the aspects of relationships, there had been many. None of these men were of character with the qualities I viewed the one would have. The one I believed would be honorable beyond measure. I had never bothered allowing a man to control my mind like they did. They held such an obsession to my mind. I was trapped into a world of thoughts and trapped into a world of drinking to make it all disappear. All those months of that year were full of my body residing on autopilot; crying and drinking night after night.

"Hope, now talk about the visions. You seem to get some clarity when we have talked before with other things. Maybe, if we talk you will find some explanation with them."

"Very funny, Sam. Look how many hours we have already voiced and circled that path."

"I know, but right now you have stopped the drinking and you maybe clearer."

"You already know the whole story, for with each man came a vision. Each one seemed to have his own movie in my mind. Now to me these were not fantasies. They could not have been, from what I observed in my mind, it was strange. Each time I met one, I would see something from another time, another life, kind of like a flashback. I was seeing them in the context of older centuries, and I was not at a state of even believing in past lives. In those visions, each man was very clear. Each time I would see a vision then I would start to observe it. The visions all had one thing in common, though, I saw myself in them. In each vision I did look different, sometimes longer hair, darker hair, etc.

The other common thread with each vision is that they all ended the same - with me taking my life. Each vision would end with that. You know how I felt about seeing all that, Sam. During these months, I would drink to block and hide from everything.

I was drinking, not eating and escaping. Remember, I was also running at the lake a lot during this time, never voicing to anyone but you on the phone. You know all about me seeing the spirits, and the occurrence of this happening at the same time. I was devastated and very scared with seeing what I did. As I saw the spirits more clearly it seemed to circle the understanding of why I was connected to these men. It seemed that it all started at the same precise time line. It feels that by this happening, many different doors opened; doors of understanding with what was inside of me. By acknowledging the spirits it made me stronger with my senses."

"Hope, I remember it all. How could I forget? I felt like I was experiencing it with you."

"And after the last one, I was getting this message:

'*I went back to mend my heart.*'

She started staring at me, and then she moved her chair closer to mine.

"What?" I asked.

"Hope, your eyes look funny. The pupils are so dilated, and they look weird."

"I am starting to feel light headed, and I am hearing something."

"What are you hearing?"

"Hold on let me focus; this is what I am hearing:

'My spirit attached itself to those men, and my soul went back to mend my heart.'

As soon as I voiced that to Sam, more things started to pour out of my mouth. I kept hearing, and then began saying:

'My soul is in limbo, my soul is in limbo.'

"What does that mean, Sam?"

"I have no idea, Hope, but I have a friend who may."

"No way, we are not sharing this with anyone, Sam!"

"Fine, but you should consider it since she is a dear friend, and I know we can trust her."

The next few days repeated itself with us. We talked about it, over and over, never tiring of talking about it. I was sleeping through the night without waking. This felt good. The darkness under my eyes started to shift and show some color. In the morning we seemed to get up at the same time, reaching the hallway together.

"You are looking alive," Sam said.

"Thanks, I feel some what different."

We decided to take some days and head to the beach. My house was only a few hours away. The ocean always has its way with soothing one's mind. It was off season, but the days were warm enough to swim.

We packed up our stuff, and headed off to the beach. After the long drive, we found a small but nice place facing the waves of the ocean. It was perfect, and we took most of the days to lay in the sun. I never would go into the water. I had a fear of the water, even though I could swim I felt like the waves wanted to take me away. Many times thinking it might be more of a blessing if the waves took me - rather than actually dealing with all the pain I was going through. Yet, I never had the nerve to test it.

We decided to go out in the evenings; dancing was still one thing I really enjoyed. One evening while out, a strange feeling started to emerge within me. My eyes started dilating, and Sam commented on it. We were talking with some people and I did not want them to notice. I went into the bathroom, hoping it would disappear. The strange feeling was always accompanied by my surroundings spinning around me. It made me feel out of control of my body. I sat in the bathroom, letting things come into my mind. Over and over I heard a voice repeating:

'You need to find him.'

"Who find who?" I asked, talking out loud to myself. *'The one,'* the voice said.

Not this again. I let the thoughts come in, and then waited for them to subside. Finally, my mind was clear and I started to feel normal again. I went out and asked Sam if she was ready to leave. I felt drained and wanted to go to sleep.

We headed back to the house and I went in the bathroom to get ready for bed. When I came out Sam was sitting on the bed, and I stopped in my tracks.

"That look - I know that look, what is it?" she said.

"I see another person next to you, a male," as I began describing him to her.

"Hope, it has to be my Uncle, my Dad's brother. The way you are describing him - it has to be him. Talk to him. Please, talk to him."

So I did communicate with her Uncle and it was a very important message for her. The message was relating to Sam's family. Much of the message related to mysteries involving how her Uncle died.

As he was fading, I noticed he left the same way the others did. He floated backwards, facing me the whole time. She was crying and I kind of felt bad, and I wanted to comfort her.

"I am sorry, Sam."

"Don't be sorry, Hope. That was amazing, thank you." she said.

In the next few days, I would tell her things that I would see. I knew things about her and my information seemed to be accurate. We spent an amazing week at the beach relaxing, laying in the sun, swimming and talking.

When we got back, we went over to Darleen's house. I wanted Darleen and her husband to meet Sam. We spent the day, and most of the evening visiting. Sharing with the three of them was easier. Talking about the supernatural incidences seemed to flow now; it was not a hidden secret anymore.

Darleen mentioned that she had found something that might interest me. It was a community that gathered together once a week. It was a spiritual community, and she suggested maybe I should look into going. I told her I would think about it. I needed some more time to process everything and be with it. She handed me a piece of paper about the community with their information on it. We had dinner with them, and then headed back in the late hours. Sam and I talked about the spiritual community, and she thought it might be a good support for me. I was also feeling a strong pull to it. I trusted that feeling, because when I started to feel things inside, I would just know.

There was a knowing without explanation, a feeling that something was resonating within the depths of me. We talked about this a lot and it made sense in many aspects. I felt I did not have a choice, I felt I should try and follow my senses and it may lead to others that could help with understanding.

"Sam, imagine all of this kept coming to me even after a whole year of drama and drinking. It is time to start acknowledging the importance of what I am experiencing. I can not use drinking to block the visions anymore. I feel I can no longer hide from knowing and sensing things strongly."

"I think you are starting to realize that you used the alcohol to escape, Hope. Maybe identifying this pattern, will keep you away from drinking." she insisted.

The days rolled by quickly and then it was time for Sam to go. It seemed like she had just arrived, yet our time and talks together presented it to be differently. We had discussed and experienced so much together during her visit. I was nervous for her to go and to be alone with myself. It had been nice to have someone to lean on - a friend who was trying to understand. While she was here, things would come to me and we would write them down. Often, after the words would come to me, I would not always remember them. We realized if she did not write down what I was saying, it might be lost.

The writings were a reminder to keep track of all that was said. We worked together talking of nothing else but what was happening to me. We filled two entire notebook's up while she was here.

She left on a Saturday afternoon and I headed right to the lake for a run. I discovered a new path. I felt pulled to go, so I began to run down the unfamiliar slope. I wound up at a stream and found a log to sit on. I sat for what felt like hours, staring into the water. Letting all thoughts come in and try to be. The sound of the water was so peaceful, and hiding in the trees felt so comforting.

I headed back down the trail to my jeep. When I got home, I began cleaning my kitchen. I was startled as I looked out the window and noticed a man walking through my backyard. All of a sudden I felt a surge of energy in my body, and I got goose bumps all over. I felt so overwhelmed that I had to stop cleaning the counter. I angled my head to see the back door, which was connected to the living room. The man floated right through the door and sat down on a chair in my living room. I freaked out, started shaking, and literally ran out the front door.

I went right over to Darleen's and told her what was happening.

"Go talk to him Hope," she said, like it was no big deal. So I asked her to come with me, and she did.

He was still sitting on the chair facing straight ahead. I sat on the couch with Darleen and said,

"This is weird." As soon as I spoke he turned and looked at me. He did not say anything, and he seemed freaked out, too.

"I think he is more freaked out then I am. I feel like he is lost and I do not know what to do," I exclaimed to Darleen.

I looked over at the chair and told the spirit I could see him. When I told him I could see him, he looked right at me, got up and went right through the door.

"What was that? I said looking to Darleen. "It did not make sense, what am I suppose to do with that?"

"There is nothing you can do."

"Great, now you have to leave, and my house is going to be full of floating spirits."

"No, I am sure it will be fine, Hope."

"Why are you not freaking out about this? You don't find it weird?"

"Come over if you get freaked out," smiling as she walked out the door.

I think that she was just trying to comfort me, and not wanting me to feel crazy.

After she left, the nights seemed to be fine and it was nice to be able to sleep again. The spirits that used to visit at night were now wandering around my house during the day. I had my nights back to myself. The fear seemed to go away, and I would write mostly poetic stuff at night. Every bit of the writing seemed to talk about love in some way. So I started voicing these poems as my "love stuff."

I found myself listening more as the voices got louder and clearer. Referring this now more as my guidance than voices in my mind. People always seem to judge and make jokes about people hearing things in their head. I stopped worrying about the fact that I was hearing the voices in my mind. This was no longer a big fear for me. The voices were there and I finally accepted that it might be valuable information.

Once I did, I would start getting things that related more to myself. I would hear things like, 'A very important girl is coming into your life.' I had no idea what that meant, but that is what I was hearing. I started taking action on the messages by doing what I was hearing. When I was told to call someone, I did. It always proved important, once I took the action.

Then one day I awoke and heard, 'Go to the community center.' I found the paper Darleen gave me with the address. I was nervous because I did not know what to expect. I managed to get dressed up, I was having a hard time functioning. The strange feelings and spinning was still a regular obstacle for me. I climbed into my jeep and sat there for a moment, wanting to cry. I took off with the directions in my hand. As I was driving I looked over at my passenger seat and my Dad was sitting there. He had passed away seven years prior.

It startled me, and I had to pull over to breathe. He did not say anything to me, and my mind was saying, 'Look at the directions.' I looked at the road that the community center was on - it was on Lee

Street. My Dad's name is Lee. Then I heard, '*Look at the date.*' It was my Dad's birthday. I thought to myself, 'these have to be good signs.'

My body seemed to be frozen, and all I really wanted was to reach over and hug him. I could not stop staring at my Dad because it had been so long since I'd wrapped my arms around him. I did not want to take my eyes off him as I was afraid he would disappear. I wanted him to tell me, "Everything will be Okay." He used say that to me when he was living. In my life if anything went wrong he would look at me, smile and say, "Everything will be Okay." This always made me feel better no matter what. His words brought calmness to me and I missed him terribly. My Dad was much older, and many of my friends thought he was my grandfather. I think this is why, I love being around older people so much. I feel they have such a wise way with them.

I pulled myself together, after sitting with the shock. I was not sure I even believed it could be my Dad next to me, but I was grateful to have his presence near me.

I found the building, and made my way inside. I wondered if it would be like Sunday's were for me when I was a child. I used to attend mass regularly growing up, but had lost my connection over the years. In this facility, there were folding chairs all aligned in rows, facing a small stage. I wanted to be by myself in the back. So, I started to head to a empty seat when a women approached me. She looked to the left of me saying, "You have an energy with you."

I thought, 'How did she know that?'

"I know. It is my Dad, and today is his birthday," I spilled the words out without even thinking first.

"Happy Birthday," she said, as she turned her head to look to the left of me.

I was shocked she sensed him, how did she know that? I realized I didn't care how, or why, it put some comfort in me. I sat down, and the man at the front began to speak. I looked over at my Dad, and he said, "This is where you need to be." Then he vanished.

"Okay, Hope, this is good. You are going to be fine." I voiced out loud to myself and then I consciously looked around to make sure no one was looking.

A middle-aged man stood on the stage wearing a Hawaiian print shirt and a headset over his ear. Looking at his casual dress made me feel welcomed. I already realized this was not my "normal" program of what a Sunday morning used to look like for me. It was crowded, but not too bad. Then all of sudden I began to cry when he started speaking. His words touched something deep inside of me. He spoke of belief, truth and trust. I grabbed a tissue and cried the entire time - he was reaching all of the emotions that I had been feeling since this first began with me. I tried to hide myself from anyone noticing all the tears running down my face.

Listening to the talk, I looked up to see a girl walking towards me. It was the girl I met when I arrived at the center. She passed by me, dropping a tissue in my lap, and a piece of paper with her name and number on it.

I left before it was over. I was afraid to talk with anyone; I could not stop crying. As I was walking towards the door of the room, I was getting, 'Turn around.' When I did, the girl that approached me in the beginning was staring back and smiling. I put my head down and walked out quickly. The talk did feel good to hear, and I knew I would be back.

I went straight to Darleen's. She had coffee waiting for me on the counter. I told her about what I had encountered that morning at the community center. She found it all fascinating, and was very support-ive. I found it very comforting to be around her. I told her about the girl, and she said I should call her. The piece of paper read, "Abigail" and had a number. I contemplated calling right then, but could not bring myself to phone her quite yet. I thanked Darleen for coffee and headed back home to take a warm bath.

The next few nights, I would wake up soaked from sweat and would vaguely remember my dreams.

I sat up one morning dripping with sweat, "Dear God, the heat is pouring out of me!" I only can only remember one thing. Each time in the dream, I would look over and in some distance a guy would be standing there. He seemed younger than I was, and his hair was about shoulder length. I don't know how I knew that, but he seemed and felt younger. I could vaguely see his face, but I kept sensing he was younger. I could not figure out why I would see him each night in my dreams - why he kept coming to me. I did not recognize him, but he was beautiful.

I called Sam the next day to fill her in on what had been happening. I voiced to her about the younger guy in my dreams.

"How do you know he is young?" She said.

"Not young like a child, just younger in age then I am. Why is he in my dreams?"

We had no idea, and I did not feel like trying to figure it out. So we let it go. I was not one to have vivid dreams. I did have them when I was a child, but they stopped suddenly. I don't remember any dreams after childhood. Now, I am waking up completely dripping, and seeing someone I don't even know. Still the dreams occurred, night after night.

I waited a few days, and then I decided to call the girl I met at the community center. Out of desperation I finally got the nerve up, sat outside and held the paper in my hand with her number. Why was this so difficult? I feel like I am stalling, yet I keep getting, 'Call her.' That unusual voice would come back, and I was hearing, 'Call her.' I was scared. What if she thinks I am crazy? 'Crazy. Oh, there is that word again.'

I dialed the number and she answered. She asked if I wanted to come over and have tea.

"Sure, where do you live?" I wrote down the address and said, "That is odd, you only live two blocks away from me."

Amazingly enough, the community center where I met her was a forty minute drive, and she lived literally, only two minutes from my home.

As I drove over, I started recalling what she looked like. She was around my age, dark hair, my height, and small build. When she looked at me it seemed that her smile had a soothing feeling to it. I recalled when she approached me smiling, my whole body calmed down. Her smile seemed to put me at ease.

I rang the door bell, and she opened the door. I walked in through the front door. A large beautiful piano sat to the right of the room and shelves lined the walls with books. The house felt warm, and very quiet. Sitting at the kitchen table, I asked,

"Do you go by Abigail, or do people call you Abbey?"

"Both, you can call me which ever one feels right."

We spent the whole day and night talking. I shared most of everything with her, and not at one point did I feel weird about it. She listened with such compassion and we instantly connected. I got ready to go and she gave me a big hug, and said, "I will see you again soon."

That night, it seemed that all the memories that I had gone through did not hurt as much. I did feel very tired. Anytime I would rethink the memories of the past couple of years, it caused exhaustion.

I headed up the stairs and on the way I noticed an image out of the corner of my eye. I ran, jumped in bed, and started to have pains in my chest. I was not able to breathe normally, and having pains a lot. I closed my eyes, and in my mind I was seeing something in my hallway. I was seeing a very tall old man, standing right in the middle down the hall. I sat up breathing so hard I felt as if I was having a heart attack. I staggered out of the bed and went downstairs, refusing to look down the hallway. On the way down, I kept getting, *'Old soul, Old soul.'*

As I was standing in the kitchen, my mind was taking in the visual of my thoughts upstairs. I said out loud, "He is standing at the core of my house."

As soon as I said that, I could feel him behind me. I refused to turn, it scared me, and I froze. My body relaxed, and I was getting, *'Kind soul.'* All of a sudden I was seeing a hand reaching for my shoulder. His hand touched my shoulder, and I could feel a coldness going right down to my heart. The pain in my heart stopped, and I was able to breathe normally again. Then he vanished and I went upstairs to go to bed. Glancing out of the corner of my eye, he was still standing in the hallway.

'What is he doing, and why is he still there?' All of a sudden, I was seeing what looked like a long rope in his hand. It was bright white and I watched as he started to lasso it. The hoop got bigger and bigger it was going around the outside of my house. When he was done, I thought, 'Yeah, tell that one to someone, Hope.'

The next day Abigail called me, and asked me if I would come over. I told her I was going over to my neighbors for a few hours and would see her after that.

I went to Darlene's, and told her about the old man. In her amazement, she asked if I got anything while he was there.

"Yes, I was getting, *'Old soul, Old soul.'*

I expressed to her about the heart pains I had been encountering.

"We called my grandfather old soul, and he was a healer," she said as she sipped her coffee.

"Weird." I told her, "I think he healed me and maybe put some kind of protection around me and the house."

I stopped and stared over at Darleen, feeling in a trance-like state.

"What is it, Hope? Do you see something?"

"It is strange, Darleen. I see bright circles in the center of your body."

"How many do you see?"

"I see seven," and pointed to the areas where I saw them.

"Hope, those are called chakras. Do you know what chakras are?"

"No, I have never heard of them. What are they?"

"I think that you will find out what they are when the time is right."

"I have to go. I'll come over again soon. Thanks for the talk." I said as I got up to leave.

I arrived at Abigail's and right away she started talking about chakras.

"Funny, Darleen and I were talking about the same thing. I was getting some things with it while I was with her, I think I saw them."

Abigail briefed me that there are seven energy centers in the body. "Hope, you can see them? Can you see mine? Can you check and see if you see mine?"

"I don't know. This is all so new to me - what do you mean check them?"

"Voice to me exactly what you see."

I thought, 'Why not?' I looked and told her I saw different colored circles, mainly within her torso. "What are the colors?" She asked in a surprised voice.

I voiced what I saw, and then told her, "A few are not lined up right. Whatever that could possibly mean."

"I will help you understand. Go with what is coming to you," she said.

So I did. It was strange seeing something new again that I had no prior knowledge about. After, we talked about everything I described what I was sensing and I seemed to be right on with the energy circles.

She told me about what she had read, and what I was voicing matched all that she knew about Chakras.

We spent many days talking, and things seemed to keep coming in for me. I was getting information and I had no idea what it meant or why. All of this knowledge was coming to me, and it was stuff she was already familiar with from the books that lined the shelves in the piano room.

When the day came to go to the community center, we decided to go together. She picked me up early so we could go eat first. I was not feeling too well. I was afraid I was falling back into a depression state again, like when I was drinking and having the obsessive visions with the men in my life. Holding her hands on the wheel, she looked over at me, "Are you okay? Do you want to talk about it?"

"No. Actually, having some food may be a good idea." I was trying to redirect the subject and I did not want to get drawn into talking about the depression state again.

Silently we ate, left the restaurant, and parked outside of the community center. We found seats and got settled. I was looking around and noticed someone. It was a young man and he was standing across the room. All of a sudden, I felt something in my gut. Even though his back was to me, he seemed familiar to me. It felt as if my body wanted to float towards him - almost as if I were being pulled to him. He turned, then the feelings magnified of familiarity. I knew him.

"Who is he?" I asked.

"Oh, that is Jesse, he comes almost every week."

There was something about him. I knew him and I could not put my finger on it. I turned around and said to Abigail, "Oh well, it probably means nothing."

The next few days, I kept running across the same flyer everywhere I went. It was a flyer for a charity run in a few weeks. The charity run was to raise money to support research regarding mental illness for children. After seeing it three times, in different locations, I grabbed the information. I went right home and called the number on the paper to see if it was too late to register. It wasn't, so I gave all my information and signed up to run.

After I hung up the phone, I was quite excited about it; especially since I had been running three times a day around the lake. My insides felt good, I wanted to do something to help. I could tell this was definitely something I was led to do. I had never heard of the place where the run was to be held, but I was sure I would find it.

I grabbed my notebook and headed to the back deck. As I was journaling, I thought about my writings, which seemed to get into more depth now. I was writing page after page, and many love poems followed right behind. I was about to stop after I had been writing for an hour, when I had the urge to flip the notebook over and write this poem:

The eyes of the night are open,
and the stars are watching over us
We beacon all hope for twilights
to see the capturing moon in its full light
His love stands in the distance
and lingers in the air
to find her heart still holds only him so dear
She captures a moment of love,
a glimpse of who it is
In the depths of shadows it is shown
a love which will only be revealed
by the sacredness of the moon

Baffled by the writings, I sat quietly. I stared at the night sky and found myself searching for the moon. I swung my chair around and found myself gazing at the moon right in front of me. Looking up I thought, 'What is it? Is there something I should know? Come on. Why the importance of this one? Who is he?' My senses were strong. All that kept coming to my mind was:

~He was the missing puzzle piece that would fit it all together.~

I thought, 'Whatever, after all that I have been through this last year. No way. I was not going to let this consume me, and take me over like it did with the other ones. I will not let those remembrances of obsessions control me again.' It was too painful, and the stories haunted me in the night. I always knew when I used the word "whatever" I was entrapped in the mindset of being angry. That word was not one of my favorites, and I did not like when it was used around me.

I started following the voices even more the next few days. One day I was getting, 'Go to the library' so I did. I didn't question; I just did it. Not knowing what I would find, I walked through the automatic doors. Looking around I thought, 'Okay this is crazy,' I was walking back through the door. Suddenly, Abigail came around the corner.

"What a surprise! Fancy meeting you here."

"Yeah, I guess," as I looked at her smiling.

"This is weird; I guess we are suppose to talk. Should we sit down?" As she pointed to an empty table.

"I made lunch before I left for the library," she said. "Let's go to my house and eat and have some more conversation."

As I was following her home, things started to come in. I pulled over and wrote down what I was getting. I did not really sit and observe the words written, I simply wrote them down. When I finished, I threw my notebook on the seat and headed to her house. I went straight into the kitchen and sat down.

"I did not stop when you pulled over, because I felt you needed to write something." she said as I arrived.

"You were right. That is what I was doing. It often happens that way and I let it come." I stared at her with an expression that seemed to catch us both off guard. I could feel she sensed my sadness; I could see it in her eyes.

"You know, I think we should go out and have coffee downtown."

"Abigail, I know that I just got here, but I think I should go home and rest. I am not in the mood to eat, or go anywhere, or really talk much for that matter. I am feeling very strange, and think I want to lie down," saying as I replied to her with a thank you.

I went right home, ran a bath, lit some candles, and found my old radio. The bath made me feel better. When I got out I realized I had been in the tub for two and half hours. I was amazed; I even thought I may have fallen asleep.

I curled up into my bed, and was laying there, not really feeling any thoughts. I fell asleep, waking with the phone ringing. Answering it, hearing:

"Good morning, Hope. How are you feeling today?"

"I don't really know. I feel tired and not so good."

Abigail's voice got louder and happier, saying "Come over - I want to share some things with you." With that I heard "Bye!" and the phone went dead.

I could barely get out of bed, taking my feet only a few steps away, I sat on the chair. What is wrong with me? I started to remember my dream from the night. In the dream, I saw lots of people and I was in a crowd. I remember standing on some grass and when I looked over I could see *him* again. At that moment I tried to make my mind focus with the dream. Who is he? I wondered, as I looked closer. I could not see him, but I felt and knew it was the same one that had been visiting my dreams before. Faintly, an image of his face appeared. But as fast as it came, it went.

I was startled by the phone again. It was Sam, and I told her about the dream.

"It is so odd. Don't you find this strange?"

"Hope, nothing is strange with you anymore," she replied with a sly tone.

"I am going to get into the shower and head over to Abigail's," laughing at her comment.

"Hold on, I want to ask you a favor. Do you think you can help me with something?"

"Like what, Sam?"

"I need you to sense something for me," her voice lowered.

"What is it, Sam?"

"My grandfather is in assisted living, and he is not doing well. My Dad called, and said I needed to come over to see my grandfather right away."

As soon as she said that, I was getting a clear image in my mind. I told her, "I can see a room," and I described it to her. She was not sure what the room looked like because she had never been there before. As I continued to describe it, she drew it out on a piece of paper.

"I think I can see your grandfather and he is sleeping."

"Do you think he is going to be alright?" She asked.

"Well, Sam, honestly I don't know. I am not getting anything. Can you call me when you get there, and maybe I will get something?"

I ran the hot water in the shower, and just stood with my head leaning against the cool tile. I got out, and headed to Abigail's.

When I got there, the door was open, so I called through the screen. She came up to the door, "You don't have to knock, come in from now on." I noticed that her house smelled of lavender as we walked to sit at the kitchen table.

"How am I to understand all of this?" I asked her.

"Why do you need to understand it all? Let it come in without analyzing it. Go with what you feel is right, and let it guide your way!"

"You don't find it odd?" I looked at her with a puzzled expression.

"No, Hope. I have been working with this kind of thing for many years now."

I told her all about the dream and the poems I had been writing.

"I bet it will make sense one day," she smiled.

After a pause she mentioned, "Tomorrow the community is meeting again and having a potluck afterwards. Do you want to go with me?"

I was getting 'Yes,' in my mind. I had started asking myself questions and would receive the answers clearly.

"I want you to do something for me," she said, as she pulled out some tarot cards.

I knew what they were. I had been to a psychic back home that used tarot cards during a reading with me. I was in my teens so I had forgotten about it until this moment. Abigail laid the tarot cards in front of me.

"Can you give me a reading?"

"What? I can't do that. I don't know how to."

"Yes, you can, try," laughing while she voiced this.

Ironically enough, I started shuffling the cards and I felt like I knew what I was doing. I had her pick a few, and then laid them on the table face up. I looked closely at them, feeling somewhat weird about what I was doing. Abigail had not told me much about her life.

"Do I just tell you what I see?" I said.

"Yes."

So, I began to tell her things and she confirmed that I was right on with my sensing. It was actually fun. As we spoke, more and more things came to my mind. Quite interestingly, I said, "Maybe I could help people. Perhaps, I could help with loved ones that have passed on. I knew the impact it had on me when my Dad passed. If I could only help people in some way, it may bring some comfort to them. I don't know if I am ready for all this, Abigail. I am not sure how I feel about people knowing this about me."

I went on, and expressed to her that many months ago, I called a woman. This woman was a psychic and I wanted to have a reading from her. I was hoping in all my confusion that she could explain what was happening and would have my answers. I remember the conversation clearly. I was speaking to a woman with an older voice. She was very hesitant and quiet with me on the phone. When I asked her how long she had been doing this, her response was, "Sweetie, a lot longer than you."

I told her I was not doing anything and she said, "I cannot help you." Then she said, "Go to the Lila Institute at the State University and they can help you. They teach about paranormal phenomenon. I feel this would be a good place for you to start. I see they will be able to give you guidance."

"You should go," Abigail voiced.

"I don't know. I am not sure that I am ready. I did look it up, and they are holding a meeting this afternoon."

"Hope, you should go. Definitely go," then she said, "Ask yourself."

When I asked myself, I was getting, '*Yes, yes,*' and it got louder. "I don't know. Can we talk about something different?"

We tried to talk about different things, but the subject kept finding its way back into the conversation.

Then my phone rang and it was Sam. I could feel her extreme excitement.

"Can you talk?" She asked.

"Sure, what's up?"

"Hope, the room! My grandfather's room," then she paused.

"What? What is it?"

"It is exactly like you saw it. Even the position of the bed is right where you described."

As we talked I could hear something, but it was very faint, so I ignored it. Then I heard it again. It was a voice coming from inside the phone, but not Sam's voice. I jumped back in shock and said, "I have to go." I hung up the phone on her.

"What happened?" Abigail asked.

I explained that I was talking to Sam, and then I heard another voice. At first I could not make it out, but then I heard it again. It was faint, but I heard '*help me.*'

"Call her back. You should call her back right now!"

I grabbed the phone and called Sam back, explaining what I heard.

"Hope, my grandfather is not responsive. He is laying here with his eyes closed."

"Sam, grab his hand and whisper in his ear. Ask him if he can hear me. I think I may be doing some kind of communication with him."

She whispered in his ear and said, "Grandpa, if you can hear Hope, squeeze my hand." He squeezed her hand! In her excitement, she dropped the phone.

"Sam, I think he is telling me something."

It was about five minutes or so before Sam said,

"Are you there?"

"Yeah, go into the hallway and I will tell you what he said. Sam, I don't know if this makes sense. Is your grandmother there?"

"Yes, she is in another room down the hall."

"Go to her, Sam."

While she was walking down the hall, I told her about the conversation with her grandfather. "Your grandfather wants you to sing a song. I have the song in my mind, but I have never heard it before."

I then tried to sing some of it to her as she walked down the hallway.

"Are you sure, Hope?"

"Yeah, that is what he said," I told her.

With some hesitation she said, "Hope, my grandmother had a stroke about five years ago. She won't understand me, she is also not responsive.

"Sam, please try."

"Okay, I will try," she sighed as she approached her room. Sam began to sing, then I could hear Sam crying as she kept singing.

Then the phone cut off, and I sat and waited. I shared what was happening to Abigail as she sat and observed. After about twenty minutes later, Sam called back crying.

"What happened?" I asked.

"When I began to sing, my grandmother sang with me. Then with tired eyes, my grandmother looked right into my eyes, Hope. She said, "baby lullaby, baby lullaby," and smiled at me." Sam was hysterical and said, "My grandmother has not smiled in five years, Hope."

According to Sam's Dad, the lullaby was from her grandmother's era. She sang it to all eight of her children when they were babies. I could feel both Sam's sadness and gratitude for what happened. I told her I would call her that night.

I felt a bit of shock when I replayed all the occurrences over in my mind. I told Abigail I was sorry, but I needed to go home. All of a sudden I was so tired that I was having a difficult time keeping my eyes open.

Once I got home, I laid down, with thoughts of knowing something else about Sam's grandfather. I was feeling he was going to pass away tomorrow and I did not want to tell Sam. How could I tell her something so sad? Even more, how do I know I am even right?

As I laid there, the front doorbell rang. I jumped up, ran down the stairs, and saw Darleen peeking in through the window. She came in and I made us some coffee, and then we sat out on the deck. I told her it was getting stronger, and that maybe I should go to the Institute the psychic woman described to me over the phone. "They have a seminar today, in about an hour."

"Let's go," Darleen replied. "You will be fine. Come on I am driving. Maybe this can help you."

She was out the door before I could even stop her. I started questioning going, but she was already pulling the car out of the driveway.

When we arrived, we sat for awhile in the parking lot. We were thirty minutes early, and I was not feeling too good. Darleen turned her head to look at me, "Do you feel we should go in?"

"I am getting '*Yes,*' but my body is opposing the answer."

"Hope, you always seem to listen, so it is settled! We go in."

We headed in, and found a room with many people sitting in it. The room had two long tables connected together with chairs all around. It was a small room and each wall was covered with layers of books. We found a seat, and I thought I was going to pass out. My body felt so heavy; like someone was sitting on top of me.

A man was standing at the front of the room and he began to speak. The topic was astral traveling. As he elaborated about it, I started to "light bulb." After each little word, it seemed like light bulbs were going off in my head. I did not know what he was saying; the topic was unfamiliar to me. Yet, what he was saying and talking about is something I had been experiencing. He was explaining my experiences.

The man began to look around, then asked, "Would anyone like to share an experience?"

Darleen kept nudging my arm, and the man looked right at me. Which lead all the eyes of everyone in the room to me? An experience arose in my mind. How do I know for sure if this is even what he is talking about? I could feel all the eyes upon me, so I decided to voice my story.

"I was on the phone with my friend one day. She was in her basement talking to me, looking for something. I had never been in her basement, but I could feel the coolness of air while we talked. The next thing I know, I could see her looking over a desk. I felt like I was standing behind her and told her, "Hey, you just moved Matt's slippers out from under the desk."

Surprised she asked, "What? How did you know that? How can you see that? Hope, you are freaking me out."

Then I could see her spin around. "I think I feel what you are looking for, and I know where it is. Look in front of you, to the right of the desk in that box."

Sure enough she found what she was looking for in the box. We both laughed, knowing these strange occurrences were becoming normal for me.

"Do you have any more of those experiences?" The man standing behind the podium, asked.

"Actually, quite a few,"

"Can you talk afterwards?" then he proceeded to speak to the group.

That was the first time I heard the word, "Astral traveling." I was happy to get an explanation. It felt good, and for a moment I did not feel crazy or afraid to share anymore. Afterwards, Darleen and I hung around, and I shared a few more stories with him.

"Do you meditate while you are doing this?" He asked me looking a little confused.

"What? No, it seems to come when it wants to. I have also had visions where I see myself in a different time and place. Many times with a Native American chief, and well... Then I stopped myself and said, "I don't know."

I was starting to feel uncomfortable. I was wondering if I was doing something wrong. Why would he ask about meditation, and why was I not meditating?

"I think I am ready, are you?" Darleen asked.

"Yeah, I am getting tired."

The man turned to me, "It was very nice meeting you. Thank you for listening. Please come back again. We are here every week."

I got home and immediately called Sam. We did not speak long since she was with her grandfather. I told her I would call her back in a few hours. I spoke to Abigail for a long time and told her everything about the Institute and apologized for heading out so quickly earlier.

"Hope, you never need to apologize for anything. It is fine and I understand. Would you still like to go with me tomorrow? Do you remember me telling you the community center is having the pot luck? If you want to go, come over around nine o'clock. We can make something together, and then head out."

"Abigail, that sounds good. I need to go now. Have a good night and see you tomorrow."

I walked down the hallway and into the bathroom. At this moment, standing in the bathroom felt safe and comfortable. This bathroom was much smaller than the one connected to my room.

I ran the water, letting the warmth hit my hand. I lit candles and put the radio on. I walked into my room and into my big bathroom to grab my robe. The shadows hit the floor from the large window facing the backyard. Nothing covered this window and only the trees could see inside. It was a very nice bathroom. The tub was twice the size as the other tub, but it just felt too big to get lost into.

I headed to the smaller bathroom and let my robe hit the ground. The cool air hit my bare skin as I sank into the water and closed my eyes. Then I let myself cry as I relaxed my mind.

Many visuals came at this time and I let my thoughts flow with it. The relaxing seemed to bring more of the visuals when I was in the warmth of the water. Some of the visuals I would share with Abigail and Sam, and some I would write down. After about an hour a visualization of Sam and her grandfather's room came to mind. I took myself out of the tub, and called her. "Hi Sam, I see your Uncle there, with your Nana, too!"

These were the same spirits that gave Sam a message when she was visiting with me. "Your Uncle is looking out the window, and now I see him by the door."

Sam told me, she was standing at the door looking down the hallway and that she didn't see anything. All of sudden I heard Sam say hello to her Dad. "Hope, my Dad is here. He is my Uncle's brother. That is why my Uncle's spirit was probably looking out the window. Why do you think my Uncle and Nana's spirits are here?"

"Maybe, your grandfather is ready to go, Sam.

"Yeah, I was feeling that. I think it is time. Thank you for talking and helping, Hope. Maybe, I should visit with my Dad now."

"Sam, I will call you in the morning. I love you."

I hung up and curled into bed, covering my head to feel the security within the blankets.

The alarm rang at 8:00 a.m. I came out of the bathroom to shut it off. I was already up and getting ready as I had not slept much. I went down to grab my coffee, and sit on the deck. As I was being bathed in the warmth of the sun, all of a sudden my body jolted up. "He passed away! Shoot!"

I ran in the house feeling my friend's sadness. I could not find the phone, where is the phone?! I ran all around searching everywhere and it felt like hours. Finally, under my bed for some reason, I could see it sticking out. I dialed, and heard a small cry on the other end. "I am sorry, Sam. If there is anything I can do."

"He passed, Hope - a few minutes ago."

I did not know what to say, so I offered, "I am sending you love. Call me when you want to talk."

"I will, Hope. Thank you so much."

I sank into my chair, and felt compassion for her. How did I know he died at that very moment? Did I know so that I could help and comfort my friend? I let the wonder go, and went back to thinking about Sam and her family.

Wow, the pain and memory of losing someone you love. The aching we feel when this happens, and the racing our minds put us through. The thoughts of every moment spent with that person, relapsing over and over in our mind. Images of the time with them, and all the events shared with that person. To now having to imagine the days without them in the physical world, my heart went out to her and her family.

Living in a world called all reality
The world of make believe
Residing in a different thought
Of what is real and what is not
Do I come to explain in this reality
And try and hope all that I conceive
Asking for guidance to direct and trust
In what I believe
Hold my head high
For I do live in a cosmic way to see

Chapter III

ONE CONVERSATION

I got myself up and left to meet Abigail. As we drove to the community center, I recounted to her what had happened this morning. As we arrived and were walking through the parking lot, my body suddenly stopped. I turned my head, and thought 'I bet this is Jesse's car.'

After listening to the talk, Abigail and I found a table to eat our potluck lunch. I found myself talking and laughing with others. Abigail looked at me and stated that someone was having a bonfire after the potluck. "Do you think you may want to go?"

"Sure, why not?"

After awhile I walked around and observed everyone. One of the girls that had been sitting at our table stopped me. She was now sitting across the room. I stopped and automatically sat down and started to talk to her. I looked over and noticed Jesse right across from me. After about ten minutes she got up, saying to me, "I will see you later at the bonfire."

"See you then. Nice talking with you."

After taking my eyes off her, I looked across the table right at Jesse. "Hi, I am Hope," reaching my hand across the table.

"Hi, I am Jesse," reaching to grab my hand.

We started to talk and the conversation flowed easily. We stood up while people began to remove the tables to clean up. I don't think we budged as everything around us was being removed.

"Are you going to the bonfire?" I asked.

"No, I have to go to work."

"Where do you work?"

"I work at the lodge next to the national park. Do you know where that is?"

"Yeah actually, I just did a charity run that started at that place," I replied.

"You did?" he said excitedly, "I did too!"

At that moment I remember passing him during the run. The only reason why I remember this is because we ran by each other in the park. The run started at his work, leading a few miles up a major highway, and then entered a national park. He was leaving the park entrance, as I had entered a few minutes before, and was heading into the park. He was running towards me, going the other direction. I had my head down while I was running, but I remember looking up, and seeing him. It was memorable because, after he passed I turned to look back at him again. Then my stomach began to tighten, and I thought he was very attractive. I could not figure out at that moment why my stomach was flipping out.

My eyes came back to focus on him at the community center. He stood staring at me, something about his eyes. I let the words come out of my mouth, "So what do you do? I mean with the ability aspect of all this."

"I guess you can say I listen to my gut," he answered looking at me funny.

"Listen to your gut, I do not understand," replying back to him.

Getting lost in my thoughts and thinking to myself, 'I thought you are supposed to listen to what your guidance is saying to you.'

At that time, I was so clueless with my awareness; I only assumed everyone listened to their guidance. Isn't this how it happens with everyone? It opens up, and you start seeing and hearing things. I thought that everyone who came to the community center had experienced the same stuff that I had. Aren't the people that come different? Aren't they all aware of these weird occurrences? So far, the ones that I had met talked about energy and spirits. It did not seem odd or misplaced when they spoke of it.

All of a sudden, I noticed the whole place was clearing out. Someone abruptly tapped Jesse on the shoulder and handed him some keys. I felt like the clock had stopped when I was talking with him and that everyone had disappeared. I was shocked to realize that others were around. I found myself helping pick up the rest of the chairs scattered throughout the room. I started looking around for Jesse; my eyes just wanted to see him again. I looked behind me, where I found him kneeling down and putting some equipment into a bag. He smiled at me while he silently mouthed, "Hi." My whole body trembled. I became nervous and turned my head -- I didn't even know how to act. Abigail approached me with a smile, "Your face is a pretty rosy red color right now."

"Funny, you are so funny. Should we start heading to the door?"

"Yeah, I am ready."

As Abigail and I stood in the parking lot, he walked over to his car. 'Interesting,' I thought, 'it was the same car that I had identified as his on my way into the building.'

Abigail and I got into her car and headed to the bonfire. This was going to be different for me. I was not normally around so many people in such a free environment. When we were all sitting around, someone asked the typical bonfire question,

"Does anyone know a good ghost story?"

Abigail looked at me and laughed. I whispered "No way. Shhh, don't say anything. I am not even close to being comfortable with voicing some of this," even though I had quite a few stories and many experiences with the spirit world. I admitted this to myself noting all my different encounters with those no longer living. Sam, Abigail, and Darleen were the only ones I shared my ghost stories with.

I asked her again, "Please do not say anything to anyone. I am not ready to explain something I can not understand."

She honored my request and I sat quietly next to her. It felt nice to get out, and to hear people be so open with their experiences. Many of the people at the bonfire give readings, talk about energy, or have some kind of gift.

I came to the understanding that gift meant, spiritual understandings; it seemed to be very open-ended. We stayed a few hours and left after the sun went down. On the drive home, she asked me about talking with Jesse. I told her he was really nice, but changed the subject really fast. It did feel like a part of me wanted to talk more about him, but I resisted it. After we pulled in my driveway, I gave her a hug and told her I would call her the next day.

I went right into call Sam. As I was telling her about Jesse, I could feel her concern. "What? What are you feeling? I can feel it Sam."

"Hope, maybe this is not a good thing right now."

"What do you mean? Come on, Sam. It is nothing."

"I can hear it in your voice. You are attracted to him."

"No, I am not. After all I have been through…? No way. He is nice, and yes very cute, but nothing more. I have my guard up, and I will keep it up."

At that moment, I got a flash in my mind. I saw Jesse as a knight in shining armor. I could only repeat "Weird," as I was telling Sam what I saw; it was quick as a flash. Then all of a sudden, I said, "NO WAY Sam, it is him!"

"Who?"

"Jesse, he is the one in my dreams. No, that is impossible. Why would he be in my dreams? What does this mean, Sam?"

"It means nothing, don't put anything into it," she began pleading with me.

"You are right; it is probably just a memory or something. I am done with all the past life guys. I was receiving that information after the last man that I met - him being the hardest of all."

"Remember what you said, Hope. You said that your heart was mended. You said to me, that you went back to those lifetimes, connected physically here to those men, and then it was mended. Your heart was hurt then, but now it is mended."

"Yeah, I know I said that and we still don't fully understand what that means. I am just saying all these things as it comes to me. Then, after I sit with it, I wonder what it all means."

"Who cares what it means? You suffered greatly and now it is done. You don't even understand what is happening to you! You are feeling crazy half the time, wondering why you are seeing all the things you are."

"Fine, I will let it pass, and will not think about it." I replied, to calm her down.

"Good, let this one be. Don't cause yourself any more pain."

I began spilling out the thoughts in my mind. "How do we know I am causing this Sam? How do we know this is not happening for a reason? After meeting each man I would have a vision.

Then for some reason, I would see the vision and it would end horribly. Each one seemed to be in a different timeline. At the end of all of them, I would take my life. Why would I see such a thing? Why would I be able to see and feel it at the same time? Is my mind making these stories up? How do you explain it, Sam? I would have the visions right after I would meet these men. Tell me, Sam, do we have any explanation for this?" I found myself getting angry as I ranted, then I began to cry.

"Sam, what is it? Please, there has to be some answers to this. For ten months, day after day, I was obsessed. For ten months, night after night, I cried. For ten months, I experienced some physical torture, and I won't go back again telling you what happened before that. I feel like I am losing it."

"Come on, Hope, try and figure out what is happening to you right now. Keep moving along so you can figure this out." She said this being compassionate and wanting to help me make sense of everything.

"I am trying, really. How do we not know, that somehow he is related to all that is unfolding?"

"I care about you and I don't want to see you get hurt anymore. You did not even see those other men coming, and look how physically and mentally challenging they were for you. You are a good person, but something is happening. You are able to help other people, so try and stay focused on that."

Sam's response was soothing, and she did care for me a great deal. "I will try and not think about it, Sam. Let's see if anything comes to me in the next couple of days. I need to go for a run now."

"You are going, now? It's late."

"I don't care. The running helps - I can sink into my music. I'll call you tomorrow."

As soon as I said that, Abigail beeped in on the other line. "Hey, are you doing Okay?"

"I am fine, getting ready to go for a run."

"Isn't it too late for that?" Giving me the same response as Sam.

"No, I like to run under the night sky. The air is different at night and it is quiet. Can I give you a call tomorrow?"

"Sure, call me in the morning."

I ran for about an hour and a half, and returned home. I laid in bed for what seemed like hours. How is it that we can let our thoughts relapse over and over, thinking about what could have been? Did I do something wrong, or was this something I was supposed to experience? In the norm of what I thought was real, did it make sense that this could happen to me? Did I let it come to this? Could I even prevent what was about to happen?

All of a sudden, I found myself in the bathroom throwing up. I laid myself on the bathroom floor, as my face and tears were searching for a place to land. The coolness of the tile started to run a calm feeling through my body.

I got up and searched my room for some of my old movies. Drowning myself into the movies helped me clear my mind. I searched until I found my favorites and watched two of them. I have a thing for medieval movies. Robin Hood and Ever After were my two favorites to escape into. The movies always seemed to end with the most amazing love. The love we all search for, that happily ever after.

Abigail called first thing in the morning, I could hardly understand her. I was barely awake. She was saying something about going to the community center in a few nights and talking about some group thing. I could only say, "Sure, why not. Can I give you a call later?" I hung up the phone, and covered my head with my blanket.

The next two days I only left the house to run. During the day my time was consumed with writing; I did not speak with anyone. In the evening on the second night Abigail called, "I will pick you up in about a half an hour, be ready," and then the phone went dead.

A half an hour, what was she talking about? Oh, the community center thing. I jumped in the shower, pulled my hair up, and then got dressed. No sooner had I put my shirt on, I heard a loud honk in the driveway. That was quick.

The car was quiet all the way to the center. Even, as we walked into find a seat. Many people were sitting in the same places they had on Sunday.

The rows were all lined up the same way and Abigail went right to the front. The crowd appeared more laid back. Everyone was dressed casually and talking amongst themselves.

A man approached the stage, and announced that someone was going to sing a song. The stage was about two feet high and not very big. Abigail and I found two seats in the second row. I felt odd; it was like sitting in the front row of class in school.

Previously, I had only sat in the back when I came to the community center.

We all sat quietly, then someone approached the stage with a guitar in his hand. It was Jesse. I could feel my whole body heat up. Then out of nowhere, I started laughing like a little school girl. Abigail looked at me and smiled.

I was mesmerized by his voice. Each tune he sang, I seemed to lose myself in his words. I kept thinking how good he was. I turned to Abigail, "He is really good!" It is like I had heard him sing before. It was familiar. I put my hand over my mouth with my head down. I did not want to laugh out loud. I had a giddy feeling in my stomach, and the laughter was coming out of nowhere. I was not laughing at his singing, I was laughing at the feeling in my body. I listened intensely and I started to feel everyone disappear again - the same feeling I had when I had spoken with him at the potluck.

After he was finished, we broke into groups and spent about forty minutes sharing things with each other. As we got out of the groups, I found myself trying to find him again. This made me feel nervous, and I asked Abigail if we could go.

"Are you Okay?"

"Yeah, if you don't mind, can we leave?"

In the car I sat quietly. I did not feel like talking. I think she was sensing it, because she did not push having a conversation. Back in my driveway, she said, "You can call me anytime, even if it is late. I am always up, Hope, and don't mind talking if you need to. Maybe you can come over tomorrow and we can talk through some things."

I took a bath, and then headed to bed. My life seemed so unreal to me. I awoke sweating, and sat straight up. When I looked at the clock, it said 1:22 a.m. Now, I was wide awake, I did not feel like staying in bed. I got up and went down the stairs, to grab some tea. The heat started seeping through the ceramic, so I cupped my mug to let my hands feel the warmth.

Through the kitchen windows I could see the night sky. Wow, the night sky was so incredible; the moon was so bright it was lighting up the yard. I took myself out the back door and sat on my lounge chair. I sat back and fell into a trance-like state, mesmerized by all the beauty that the sky held. All of a sudden, I was getting, '*You need to talk to him.*' I was sensing it, and hearing it, '*You need to tell him everything.*' What, I needed to talk to him? Then I saw Jesse's face in my mind. Come on. Why? Again I was hearing, '*You need to tell him everything.*'

Out of all the encounters of the other men I never voiced anything. I never told any of them my experiences, or what was happening to me. I kept it to myself. I never shared one word. So, why him, and why now?

Even when I was out at the clubs, I kept my surreal world to myself. Going out let me escape into a different place, and I never told anyone anything. This was the one thing I could run to and hide from all of this. I would hide behind myself, and let the pain sink into the alcohol.

I was at this moment resisting with words that seem to be coming into my mind. No, I thought, not again, '*You need to tell him everything to move on.*' Move on to what? Why? Fine - move on. If that is all it takes to move on, then fine.

I sat laughing at myself. I was literally on my deck talking to myself. Great, now they are going to lock me up for sure. I went upstairs, threw myself back into bed and went to sleep.

I finally woke up and looked over at the clock. I could not believe the time. It was past one in the afternoon. I had slept a long time. I got up and took a shower, then headed over to Abigail's. I did not bother calling her first. I went over and the door was open, so I walked in. I could hear a voice from around the corner,

"AHH, you finally woke up, huh?"

"How did you know?"

"I knew you needed the rest."

I was hesitant to share with her about my past. I really did not want to be voicing it, memories too painful to even say. Now with all these things coming in with Jesse, what was I to do?

"You know, Abigail, I think I can make my own man-made pond with all the crying I have done." I said rubbing my eyes.

Abigail started laughing, "I am sorry. I just had a visual of you trying to fill a pond up with all your tears. Then all the beautiful ducks can come and bask in your sadness."

"Pretty ridiculous isn't it," as I started laughing.

"Yeah, so let's try and find something we can do today to be grateful."

"Sounds good to me. A day of gratitude."

"Hey, I know what we should do. I want to go shopping. We can have a girls' day out."

"Honestly, Abigail, I really don't like being in the malls anymore."

Abigail, showing big relief on her face, "Good, me either! Well then, why don't we go out for dinner, then maybe a movie? We can have a girls' night out instead of a girls' day out.

"That sounds great. I have not been to the movies in a very long time."

I pulled out some of my writings and asked if she wanted to hear them. She seemed very intrigued to hear what I had written. For the next few hours, I recited some of my words. Not much of it made sense. Much of it was paragraphs or statements. It was like reading a riddle, or trying to figure out a puzzle. I was finding a lot of the writings stating the word "you" and as I read on, I noticed it more and more.

"You know it sounds like you are channeling," Abigail said.

"I am doing what? What does that mean?"

"It means you are receiving and listening to information coming from someone or somewhere else. When you write like that sometimes it is called, Automatic writing."

"You mean Atomic writing? I don't know why I asked that. I had never even heard of the word, and now I was quoting it a different way than you are. I feel like I am getting something:

Atomic writing:

'*Letting your hand write freely, or writing what message you are hearing.*'

When it sank in, I exclaimed, "Cool, I guess I should go back and really read some of this stuff. Maybe, it will give me some answers to some things."

She went into her room, so she could get ready to go to dinner.

As we headed towards town, we seemed to not lack on any part of being able to have a conversation. The words and statements seemed to come out more each time we were together.

"Abigail, sometimes I wish I could feel better. Or, sometimes I wish I could disappear. I really cannot understand the whole point in all of this. What am I suppose to do with it?"

She looked at me, "Try not to figure it all out at once, let it open as it will. Try to go with the flow of it; something important seems to be emerging. Let it be and I think it will come to you when you are ready."

"I know. That feels right, and seems to be the right explanation."

"Let's go and have some sushi. Sushi sounds really good."

I turned to her, "I have never had sushi before."

"You haven't?" She asked surprised.

"No, I never really tried it."

"Tonight you will. I love sushi and cannot wait for you to try it."

The restaurant lights were really dim and not many people occupied the seating. I liked it more like this, very quiet, and lately my eyes seemed to be sensitive to bright lights. We sat quietly, and I really enjoyed the food. I ate and ate, "I can't believe how much I am eating."

Her eyes were wide, "I know, you keep going."

"I guess maybe it is because I haven't been eating. It tastes good, and I seem to be able to feel what I am eating. I can actually feel the food as I put it in my mouth. It is like I have never eaten before."

After dinner we headed to the movies, "Please, no love stories. I can only handle certain movies right now. Let's see a comedy - something that will make us laugh."

She agreed, without any hesitation. She seems to go with the flow of everything.

It was pretty late when the movie ended, but we decided to go have a coffee. As we were driving, something was coming to me. I was visualizing something and I did not know what it was.

Abigail pulled over to focus on what I was saying. It seemed very faint. I could see a Native American man. He was older and I could see him plain as day. I even noticed the depth of his eyes. He had long grey hair, and was sitting grasping something in his hand. Then the image vanished quickly. But, it was extremely clear for a split second.

"Abigail, what was that? It seemed so real, and it felt like I was there. Many times like it did when I had the visions long ago."

"What visions, Hope? When did you have them?"

I told her, "Let's go get coffee. I will tell you some more about it." It felt nice to be around Abigail, I was able to be myself even when the weird things would come into my awareness.

I shared with her all the encounters with the men. The visions, what happen to me physically, everything. I could see a tear go down her cheek, "I am so sorry, Hope."

"Don't be sorry. It happened, and it is done. I am getting it strong that I have mended my heart. Time to move on, then I told her about being led to share everything with Jesse.

She asked, "Are you going to talk to him? Are you going to tell him?"

"I don't know. I don't want anymore drama. Supposedly, I am done with all the past lives, so that feels good. I have no idea why I need to talk to him and share my experiences. When I see him, if it is still persistent and the message gets louder, I won't resist it. I mean, if I hear it loud and clear, and it is coming in that I should talk to him, then I will. I have a feeling I will see him in a few days at the community center. So, I will see what happens and not think about it until then."

We finished our coffee and left. When I got home all the stuff was still lingering around me about what I had told Abigail. The thoughts came in strong and seemed to resonate with me. My life at this point seemed so complex. I was not doing anything. I was not working; I was simply trying to survive day after day to understand. I was not contributing to my outside environment. My world seemed like a hidden secret - a life internal. Each day felt like it lasted months with all the events that had been arising. Especially, with all the spirits appearing more and more everywhere.

I met a few people that I was able to communicate this blind awareness with. I called them daily to help me keep my sanity.

Then, I had my neighbor, Darleen, who I still would visit daily. She seemed more and more intrigued with all of this.

I felt maybe, if I understood it more, then maybe I could help others in some way. Surely this knowledge had to be leading me somewhere to assist other people. Can I really take this understanding and bring it around me in a practical way?

I was still getting the message to put the books down, and not to read them. How was I supposed to understand what I was going through? Every time Abigail would bring up a workshop or seminar relating to all this knowledge, I would get a loud 'NO.' So, in the physical way of being, how was I to process all of this when I could only rely on my inner guidance to make sense of all this? I wanted to be in a space of not analyzing everything day after day. It was tiring, but I found myself not being able to stop my analytic thoughts about such a phenomenal process.

The next day Abigail called me. She said her friend Lisa was over and wanted to ask me something. I got up, dressed and headed Abigail's way. Her friend Lisa was sitting at the kitchen table. She voiced to me that when she moved near an object, sometimes it would fall on its own.

She put her purse on the table to show me what she was talking about. Then she moved closer to it, and the purse fell right to the floor with a thump.

"Can you sense anything?" Abigail asked.

Right away Lisa's chakras visually came to me. I looked at both of them and stated, "The thing that is popping up for me is her chakras." I looked over at Abigail and voiced the colors of each one. "I am sensing that her energy is twisted. Actually, I am getting her energy is backwards. I have no idea what that means, but that is what I am getting."

"Hope, can you see where her chakras are?"

"Yes, but they don't seem to be straight. When I have seen the chakras before, they line up, right in the middle of your body." I leaned over to Abigail, and said, "A couple of them are not lined up."

"Do you know which ones?"

I voiced to her that yellow one was a little to the right and that the green one was to the left.

"Hope, do you think you can walk her through aligning them back?"

"I suppose…" I closed my eyes and voiced what I heard.

Abigail helped me with the visuals of what I was seeing so that we could all work through it together. The voices were coming through to me with all indication of how the process of aligning and fixing the chakras could occur. I opened my eyes and thought, 'Wow, this is coming in so clear.' I looked over at Lisa and I could see lines radiating from her. I assumed this was her energy. All of a sudden, the lines were shifting as if the polarity of her energy had flipped. I was actually seeing the lines flip from close to her body to the farthest point away and rotate around her. "Let me know if you feel any different and if things stop falling around you." She thanked me, and I headed back home to rest.

The next few days more awareness with chakras channeled through and I would log the information in my notebook. Her friend Lisa called, and told Abigail to tell me she felt great and that objects were no longer moving on their own in her presence. I told Abigail that I was glad that it helped her, but also it was building my own confidence and trust with the voices that guided me.

After Lisa, I began working with Abigail and a few more of her friends.

It came time to go to the community center again and I told Abigail I would meet her there. I wanted to handle a few things in town afterwards, so I drove separately. Plus, I thought if I wanted to head out early I could just leave.

We sat in the middle row, and I did not notice Jesse. Ten minutes into the talk, I felt something behind me. It felt like I was sensing something familiar and it was growing stronger. I felt like I should turn around, so I did. As I slowly turned, I saw him sitting in the back row. I turned back around. How do I keep feeling things with him? Maybe, it is just coincidence. Then it started, I could hear something telling me to talk to him. It was definitely louder and it kept repeating over and over.

'*Talk to him, tell him everything so you can move on.*'

At the end of the talk, I grabbed my chair and folded it up. Each week everyone folded their chairs and placed them against the wall. I spotted Jesse standing next to the chairs stacked against the wall.

I was so nervous I thought I could throw up. I closed my eyes and said to myself, 'Breathe.' All I have to do is ask him if I can have a few hours to tell him something. I only need one conversation. That is it. I walked right up to him and said "Hi. I wanted to ask you if it is possible to get together for a few hours. I am being guided to tell you something. I am not sure why; I just know I need to talk with you. It feels strong and I think that it will help me move on. I am not sure if this even makes sense to you, but I want to keep following my guidance."

"Sure," he said smiling, "When?"

"Why not now?" I suggested.

"Hold on," he walked away and approached one of his friends, turned back and said, "I'll be right back."

I took myself over to the stage, and sat down with a group of people. He came over to me and said, "Okay, now would be good." We exchanged phone numbers while we were standing together. Then he kissed me on the cheek, walked away and jumped right into a flip across the room. I sat staring, thinking he seemed so alive, so free...

Walking outside he approached me, and said,

"I need to do something first, but can we figure out how to make this work?"

As we talked, it just seemed to not be working out that we could meet. I told him to forget it, it wasn't that important. I did not want to stand there and make it happen. I had already been through enough to have to do that. I started to walk away and said to him, "I will see you later."

All that kept running through my head was that this is way too much drama. I cannot deal with anymore drama in my life. He stopped me and said, "Tuesday, 1:00 can you meet then?"

I turned and said, "Fine, I will call you and see you on Tuesday." I turned and walked away.

I kept thinking, 'Why does this seem so hard? Maybe I am resisting this - it is only one conversation. I am not willing to let anymore drama in my life right now.'

I got home and did my normal thing: got coffee, stepped out onto the deck with phone in hand. I knew I would not get Sam's voicemail because she always seemed to pick up when I needed her. When she answered, I said, "I knew you would be home. I ran into Jesse today."

"Yeah, and what happened."

"It was weird Sam. Well, I guess not too weird. I asked him to meet with me after it came in strongly to have a conversation with him. I don't have a clue why, I just know I need to do this. I need to move on, and for some reason I need to tell him everything. I feel really strange right now - dizzy. I feel like I am getting something."

Concerned, she asked, "What are you getting?"

"I am getting, '*He will be my biggest challenge.*'"

"What does that mean?"

"I have no idea, Hope."

"Sam it is coming in strong, '*He will be my biggest challenge.*'"

"Don't think about it, try not to analyze it, go with it."

Frustrated, I moaned, "I have already had so many challenges, and I don't even feel like myself anymore. I feel weird all the time, and things keep coming in.

It seems all I am doing these days is writing. None of this even makes sense. I am going crazy, aren't I?"

"No, you are just going through something. You will be fine, I know it. Hope, you are such a good person - remember that. I feel like you lost that. I feel like you let all those men and what happened with them affect you."

"I know, but my heart is mended - whatever that means. I feel like we are going around and around with this conversation. If I can move on, then it will figure itself out. I am getting something again, Sam.

"What is it?"

"I am getting:

-He is the piece of your puzzle, you have been looking for.-

"You know Sam; I have stated over the months that this seemed like a puzzle. Maybe, this will give me the answers. Maybe he will understand."

"Hope, don't do this to yourself, he is younger than you are."

"I know. I wish I could understand where this is taking me. How is it possible that I am seeing and communicating with spirits and seeing the things that I do?"

Doing the best she could to reassure me Sam said, "Remember, who cares right now. Try and take the days as they come."

I was growing frustrated, "It is easy for you to say. You are not the one feeling crazy. I can't do this anymore, Sam!"

"I think at this point, you don't have much of a choice."

"Great. That is a great answer." My voice was getting irritated with her.

"I am so sorry, Sam."

"I know. It is fine. Don't be sorry, Hope. It is not like you to get angry. Right now, you have every right to be angry with everything that has happened, and is happening."

"Thanks, I love ya!" with that we said good-bye and hung up.

Wanting to lay down, I went into the house. I climbed up five steps, sat down, and started to cry. I should just sleep all this off. As I walked up the rest of the stairs, I asked myself if I was depressed. A loud 'NO' came into mind. If I am not depressed then what is this? I feel so non-coherent all the time.

I went to sleep, the next thing I knew my doorbell was ringing. Abigail walked right in, and sat on the couch before I even got down the stairs. I turned the corner facing her, "Hi, what's going on?"

"I felt I should come over to see how you are doing?"

"You always seem to know when something major is up with me. How do you do that?"

"I don't know. I wanted to check in, I guess."

"Oh, I am fine; I took a nap is all." I glanced out the window, "Why is it so dark?"

"Hope, it is 8:00 in the evening!" she quickly replied.

"You're kidding me. No way! I have slept that long? How is that even possible? Wow. I feel really great, though, and strong for some reason. Let me run outside and get some logs and I will start a fire for us. Do you want something to drink?"

"Sure, do you have any tea?"

"Yeah, I have quite a few varieties. They are in the right hand cabinet. Pick which one you want and I will put the water on."

I grabbed the logs, started the fire, and we sat on the floor. "I am going to talk to Jesse in a few days." I was getting, *'You need to so that you can move on.'*

"That sounds great, Hope, and very positive."

"Yeah, it seems fine and it really feels like it is supposed to happen, so we shall see… So much of what has happened seems to have consumed me. I am trying to take it all in, and now let it be."

"Have you seen any more spirits?" Asking me with a curious look on her face.

"Yeah, and I have a strange one. It is a long story so I won't get into all the details, but I saw this spirit for awhile in my house. I would just see him standing and staring at me. Finally, one day he told me to call my neighbor. So when I did, I told her what I was seeing. She dropped the phone, and told me it had to be her husband she lost many years ago. Anyways, he is around all the time now. I see his spirit, and communicate with him. He has taught me a few awareness things with spirits. I learned from him how to ask a spirit to leave. He told me what to do if I did not want to acknowledge a spirit. It seems like he is some kind of teacher right now for me. He is always around and I see him quite often. Then my friend, Sam, contacted me because she had a few friends feeling spirits around them. I called her friends and sensed for them, verifying for them that, yes, they did have spirits of past loved ones around them."

"You did it over the phone?"

"Yeah, I could see the spirit and I related the message to whoever was on the phone. It was kind of interesting, and seemed to be right on. At first, I thought maybe I was making it up. Then, I was told things from the spirit about that person. The messages from the spirits matched with that person. So, I was going with it and relaying the information. It seemed to really help the person that I talked to. I can really respect the messages coming through. I feel the loss for the person and I can feel the respect from the loved ones on the other side. Not only was I doing it over the phone with strangers, but I have done a few calls with friends back home. It seems to keep coming up, so I try and go with it."

"I am so amazed you can do this over the phone."

"I know, and it comes in clear. It is exactly like when I am in front of a person. It really seems to be helping and making me stronger with my senses."

"I can feel this means a lot to you. I sense so much compassion coming out of you for it."

I paused for a minute remembering my past, then kept voicing to her, "I lost my Dad eight years ago. I arrived two minutes after he died in the hospital. I did not get to say good-bye to him because of two minutes. I was really close to my Dad, so it hit me hard. I felt so much loss after that. I can honestly say I know how a person feels to lose someone they love. Saying good-bye is a hard thing. I think it was even harder for me, because I was so close and did not get to say good-bye. So, I guess I can feel some peace of understanding with the person that I am sensing for. Most of them cry after I talk to them, but they are so grateful. If I can help, then I want to - even if it only gives them a small amount of peace. I would have given anything for that small amount of peace with my Dad…" My voice trailed off.

Looking at me intensely, Abigail asked, "How do you feel about that now, Hope?"

"Actually to be honest, I have seen my Dad's spirit. My Dad came with me when I first came to the community center. I felt comforted by that. I stopped searching for the one thing I wanted with him, which was to say good-bye. I have come to peace with it. Maybe, now it will lead the way for me to help others find a small comfort for themselves."

"I have a strong faith in you, and I know it will happen. Keep trusting. Have you sensed or seen anything else?"

"Yes, and I will try keeping the faith. As for the rest, you seem to know most of it."

"Have you tried to read any more books?"

"Yeah, but I still get, '*Put it down*,' really loudly. I don't fight it at this point; why bother? I don't even know if I can read something that will explain exactly what I am going through."

Changing the subject slightly Abigail asked, "What time are you going over to Jesse's?"

"1:00 on Tuesday."

"Do you have any idea what you are going to say?"

"Not really. All I know is that I am supposed to tell him everything that has happened. What about watching that movie now, Abigail?"

She looked at me seriously, "You really don't want to touch the subject with Jesse, do you, Hope?"

"I don't want to make too much out of it. I only need to have a conversation with him."

"Sounds fair. You really have been through so much with all those different men. If you ever want to talk, I am here to listen."

"Thanks, Abigail. I am grateful to have you in my life."

With that, our attention turned to something much lighter, and I voiced to her, "Let me see what movies I have. This may keep our minds in a good space."When the movie was over she gave me a hug, and was going to head home. As she was walking out the door, she said, "How about you come over after your Big Conversation on Tuesday?" Looking at me with a grin.

"Funny. I am not sure how long I will be, but I will come over right after the Big Conversation."

With a knowing in her voice she said, "See you then. Have a good night and good day tomorrow."

The next day I felt great. I worked in the yard, set mulch down and trimmed the bushes. Then I laid myself down on the front lawn. Laying in the yard, my mind started racing again. I ran in the house and grabbed my notebook. I wrote for about three hours nonstop. It felt so good, that I wanted to spin in circles and dance around my front yard.

I ran back inside for a moment. When I looked out the window, I noticed it had begun to rain. I went back outside and stood with my head pointing up towards the sky.

I stood silently as the rain ran down my skin. What a feeling, it felt like little kisses all over my face. It reminded me of the tears that had been streaming out of my eyes. Yet, I took that moment to shift my thoughts and imagined it was beautiful kisses all over me instead of tears.

I enjoyed the rest of the night. When I woke up in the morning, I got ready to go meet Jesse. I called him for directions. He lived about thirty minutes from me. I grabbed lunch and headed over.

As I was driving, I was trying to get my thoughts clear. I did not want to analyze it too much.

I only knew what I was guided to do. Everything else I have been guided to do, leads me further. That is what I hoped it was doing. It felt that way. For some reason, it was very important that I talk with him. If I am done with the past lives, and if my heart is mended, then this must be the last phase of all that. I think I need to voice to him about all the men and what happened. Then maybe, that phase will release and it will be done.

Maybe, he is supposed to help me with something? There I go analyzing it again. Being so much in my head started to make me feel nervous. What if he thinks I am so completely out there? I have not shared this with any of the other guys; not once did I bring it up. Oh well. I don't know the reason. I need to stop caring about the reason and do it.

I pulled into his parking lot, and found his apartment number. His place was surrounded by trees and I loved the feeling of it. So much green surrounded the area; I walked up admiring each step of the way.

I knocked on the door, and he answered. As I walked in, the first thing that caught my eye was writing all over the walls. Literally, ink marks of words covered the plaster. I found it intriguing that he was compelled to write his thoughts down wherever he could. He had written little sayings all over the walls; there were quotes everywhere. It was amazing. All I could think of was how this is what I have been doing - writing quotes wherever I could find space to do so. I had been writing all over everything and anything I could get my hands on. It really struck me, and in some small way made me feel comforted. I sat down at his kitchen table and he sat across from me. I started to feel strange; I did not even know where to start.

So, I started with "this is very weird for me, and I have no idea why I need to tell you all of this."

He looked at me and said, "Go for it."

I started by telling him all about what was happening to me - even the part with all the men I believed were from past lives. The only thing I left out was all of the physical abuse and pain that accompanied it. I felt like crying, but controlled my emotions. I did not know him, and felt it would be embarrassing if I started to cry. Granted, a small part of me felt like I had known him for years. I felt like we have had many conversations together. It felt like we were continuing right where we left off.

I looked over at him and said, "I run a lot it helps."

"It is kind of like a pain reliever," he smiled.

"Exactly! That is what it is like! All this may seem crazy to you. It feels that way to me most of the time. I even started seeing something in my neighbor's body she called, chakras."

He pointed to something hanging in his hallway. I turned my head to see a cloth banner hanging with the chakras on it and I said excitedly, "That is exactly what I have been seeing."

We continued to talk. Well, actually, I talked and he listened. After about an hour and a half, he said, "I need to get ready soon to go meet my Dad to run."

"You run with your Dad?"

"Yeah, we run together every week."

I thought, 'I am impressed he spends time with his family like that. I like the fact that he seemed to have a good bond with his Dad.'

"We don't have to rush, but I told him I would be over at 3:00. Can you see what time it is?"

I looked at the microwave and told him it said "2:22."

He smiled, and voiced, "Great number."

I had no idea what he was talking about. A few minutes passed and I said, "I should go. Thanks for listening and letting me share all of this with you."

He began to talk, as we both walked out the door. "If anything comes to you, call me anytime. I usually don't sleep, and I am up all the time."

"Really? Me too, I don't sleep much either! Well, I have been doing better lately."

"If you need to talk, you can call. Really, if anything comes to you, call," he repeated again.

"Okay, I will." Then I began thinking, 'I can't call him. It would not make sense to. I did what I was supposed to, so that should be it, right?' I found myself not wanting to look at him too much. I did not want to be attracted to him. I knew it could only result in hurt.

"Can I give you a hug?" He asked.

"Sure."

As I approached him, he stopped and said, "Left side."

"What?" I stepped back and said.

"I always hug from the left side. It is closest to the heart."

"Really that is interesting to me," I replied.

"Why?"

"Well, whenever I have seen a spirit next to someone, it has always been on their left side. Then one day I was trying to sense why and was getting, *'It is because it is closest to the heart.'* It made me realize that I was seeing past loved ones that were close to these people. They lost someone so dearly to them. By the spirit being to their left, it was closest to their heart. This was a sign to me of a strong bond. The heart being the strongest bond of love," I smiled and walked away, heading towards my jeep.

"Hey, one more thing," he yelled as he approached his car.

"Yeah," I said, turning towards him.

"My place is always unlocked if you ever need to come over and chill."

"Thanks," waving and turning back around.

He waved, pulling out of the parking lot. As soon as I sat in the jeep, I began to feel something. It felt funny, and I don't think I have ever had this feeling. I sat for a moment and tried to experience the feeling. Then all of a sudden, I kept getting a movie in my mind. It was "Serendipity," one of my favorites, it was a love story. Why would that come in? I was feeling like my entire insides had vanished. My gut started to flip out, and I felt like I was in a fog. It was like a daze and I didn't understand this new feeling. Weird, voicing to myself. I started the ignition and drove off realizing I had gone the wrong way. I turned around in the next available parking lot. I was thinking, 'I should have asked him if he is going to the bonfire Thursday.'

As I was approaching the light I noticed him a few cars ahead of me to the right. The light turned red, and now we were side by side. I rolled down the window, and yelled, "Are you going to the bonfire Thursday?"

He hesitated, looking like he was about to say No, then said, "Yeah, after work."

The light turned green, he motioned for me to call him, and then we drove off. I looked over at the date. Today was the 22nd of November, making it 11/22. Another 22, how interesting. I wonder what that meant. Jesse mentioned 22 being a good number.

I can hold you in my arms
I can hold you all night long
Hold me dear forever true
I will always love you
Hold me dear, now hold me tight
Hold me under the moon light
Want to know that I'll be soon
I'll be soon right next to you
Waiting all this time to make it true
So hear me now calling you, hear me say how much I love you
Wait for me, I will be soon
I will come to walk next to you

Chapter IV

THIS CAN'T BE, ONCE AGAIN IT BEGINS

Sam was curious to hear about the conversation. I called to tell her and she said, "Hope, don't you find some of this odd?"

"Why?"

"Remember, what you wrote?

"Are you talking about what I sensed and heard?"

"Yes. I'm talking about the final one, the statement you shared with me a million times."

"I remember, Sam, this was it:

'The last and final one, by having a conversation with him would change the person you used to be to the person you needed to be.'

"So, Sam, how can we justify any of that? That may not mean anything; you know how this has been working. It is like a puzzle and riddles all of the time. Maybe, that conversation with him will help me grow. Maybe, this is what was needed, and that is it."

"I don't know, Hope. Something about it feels stronger."

"Yeah, I am feeling that, too. But not knowing is best right now. Let's flow with it. You're the one that told me to stop analyzing it and to let it flow. I know I want all the answers and understanding, but I am trying to trust what happens with him is supposed to."

"I know I told you to flow with it, Hope. But you get so excited when you talk about him."

Defensively, I said, "That means nothing. So what? I am not going to get wrapped up in this one. It feels different than the others and I am way too tired to let all that happen again."

"Hope, I am sorry that I am saying this, but you were so obsessed -- remember?"

"I know, and that was hard. I can't explain it. I was obsessed knowing and sensing I needed to find him - the one. I kept thinking each one of those men were the one. Then, when I let all the thoughts go of finding the one, suddenly, out of nowhere, Jesse came into my life. But, I am stronger now, and finally feel that. Trust me, Sam, I will be careful and keep a strong guard up."

With nothing else for Sam to say about that, she said, "Alright. You know I am here if you need to talk."

I began to laugh, "You are funny, we talk like 24 hours a day. So yes, my dear friend, I know you are there."

Hanging up the phone, I went back to my writings. I grabbed my notebook and read what I wrote. She was right, word for word. Hmmm, well, that still means nothing. But the last part of the statement could mean something. Who am I going to be? I closed the notebook, and pushed it aside.

The bonfire was the day after tomorrow, and Abigail said we were staying the night. She had a tent, and we could camp out. With it being still cold at night, I decided to go to the store the next day and buy some long johns. I called Abigail to see if she wanted to go.

"Yeah, I want to go. I have been waiting to hear about the conversation," she said excitedly.

When I picked her up, she was grinning from ear to ear. "What? Why are you smiling like that?"

"Well... What happened?"

"Nothing happened. I told him in length about the last months and expressed some of the things that were occurring in my life."

"That's it?" Her voice sounded disappointed.

"Why the fuss?"

"I don't know, Hope. It seemed like the right thing for you to do, I guess. You were guided to have a conversation with him. I'm just surprised you are not more excited about your talk with him."

"Not you, too. Sam already mentioned the conversation thing to me. I guess I can understand why the two of you would think this was a link for me somehow. It does seem odd, I guess. All I am saying, Abigail, is so what? He listened, that is all. I did like talking to him, though. He really listened and that was nice. He did not seem to judge anything. That felt really good. I did not feel crazy at all around him."

She looked at me and asked, "Are you interested in him?"

"What difference does it make? I don't think that is what the conversation was about. So why go there? Why bother trying to be attracted to someone that may not return my feelings?" I think she picked up on my frustration.

"Fine, we can stop talking about it. You seem to glow when you mention him is all!"

"Why does everyone keep saying that? Sam even sensed I get excited when I talk about him. Is it that obvious? I must be pretty easy to read. No, it is nothing. I am done with all the pain; I don't want it anymore."

"Do you still want to go to the bonfire, Hope?"

"Yes. And what is wrong with wanting to be around him? It feels comfortable and I can't explain that. So yes, let's go to the bonfire and have some fun. I don't even remember what the word "fun" means anymore. So I want to have some of that fun for once. At least I don't feel like I have to hide what is happening to me anymore and that feels great." We faded off the subject, and chatted until we arrived at the store.

After shopping, I got home and laid in the grass. I wanted to call him but it seemed too quick. The anticipation in my body was not happening like it was with the others. You know what? I don't care. He said I could call him anytime. I will prove to myself that this is not like the others. With him it does feel safe. So I dialed the number, and he answered.

"Hey, I was about to finish up with some friends can I call you right back?"

"Sure, but it is not important, I just called to say,

Hi." I started to regret calling him, and hesitated to answer the call back. What was I doing? I felt like I was going against all my words. I felt drawn to pick up anyways, and we began to talk.

I told him about attaching myself to all these men. I was sensing that my spirit was attaching to them; that is how I knew what they were thinking and when they were thinking of me.

"Did you know I was talking about you this morning?" He asked.

"No. I didn't pick up on that."

"Really, you didn't pick up on that? Hmm so, why were you attaching yourself to those men?"

"I don't know. That is what I was getting. I have no idea what it means. I was trying to process it, as it was happening. That is all that was coming to me, about attachment."

He voiced some words relating to attachment, and it made sense to me. For some reason I felt he understood everything I was saying. It felt so good to be open with him. It was new for me to be open to a guy, and I liked that he was responsive. We started to talk about the bonfire. I asked him, "Are you tenting out tomorrow night?"

"Yeah, you know what? I think I can do that! It sounds good."

"Cool," I got quiet for a moment. "You know what? To be honest, I am often honest. I don't like to lie. I don't know what is happening to me in reality. I am trying to be as honest as I can with what I am feeling and what I am going through."

He laughed, and said "You know what… honesty is reality."

"I really like that, see you tomorrow."

We said goodbye, and hung up. I sat staring at the trees. Why do the things he says seem to resonate with me? Again, it feels like I have had a million conversations with him. I dragged myself inside, ate, watched a movie then went to bed.

The day of the bonfire, Abigail and I spent the whole day in my yard.

"This feels so good to be outside, doesn't it, Hope?"

"Yeah, it does - it feels soothing. I love feeling the coolness of dirt in my hands, with the surrounding of nature all around me feels peaceful. The sunshine giving me warmth, the smell of the pine tress, being in the yard brings so many elements of making me feel good. Abigail, maybe this can all be a positive thing that I am experiencing. I feel I

can work through this. It will sort itself out, I know it will. I will work
on voicing it being positive as much as I can."

We went inside and washed up. She grabbed her stuff and said, "I
will be back in about two hours to pick you up. Be ready, and if you
want to make something to share that is fine, too."
I went inside, packed up some things and made a salad to bring.
I wonder if I want to have a drink tonight. I know how that makes
everything disappear. It may make the night easier if I was drinking. I
got everything ready and put things in a cooler bag and waited on the
porch for Abigail. Her lights pulled up in the driveway, and I got in. I
looked over at her, "I think I want to drive. Do you mind?"
"No, if you are feeling that, it is fine with me." So we loaded everything up, and got into my jeep.
"Are you excited to have a fun night?"
"Sure, let's go do it."

It took us about an hour to get there. The old farmhouse with the
long, wooden front porch was set back from the road. It was out in the
middle of nowhere, a far view from any other homes. There were giant
trees all around the farm and a large forest area around the perimeter.
We parked behind a row of cars, and could see a faint beam of light
coming from the backyard.
"That is probably where everyone is right now!" Abigail pointed to
the back.
We took the stuff inside and headed to the backyard. Jesse was not
around, yet. His friend Dean walked by me, and said, "Jesse is on his
way." I had only met Dean one time at the center. So I did not feel I
could stop him and start a conversation. His was tall like Jesse and had
the same dreamy look to him. I smiled, and said "thanks."
Then, a girl I had never seen before walked up to me asking, "What
are you all about?"
I did not know how to respond to her bold question. I wondered
if she was a friend of Jesse's. I told her some things about myself, and
then I looked over and noticed an older man. I could sense some spirits around him, so I walked over to him. I put my hand out and said,
"Hi, my name is Hope."
He returned a hand and said, "My name is Tim."

I was straight forward with him which I normally don't do, and said, "You know, you have some spirits around you."

His eyes got wide and said "I know. I feel them." I did not saying anything more, but was sensing some musician type energy.

"Can you see them?" He asked.

"I can feel them, but I need your permission to see them."

"I would love for you to do that. Maybe, we can get together one day and see what comes through."

Abigail was calling me from the distance, so I told him I had to go. "It was nice to meet you, Tim."

"Hey, Hope - I feel like they are some kind of musicians, does that sound right?"

I was walking across the yard and said, "Yeah, that does."

I was heading towards Abigail when she looked towards the front of the house. I looked over and Jesse was getting out of his car. He drove a vintage car, I love vintage cars. I don't know something about vintage was fascinating to me. I waited a few moments, and walked over to him. My insides felt like it was bouncing all over the place. I seemed to be getting excited as I took each step closure to him.

"Hi," I said quickly.

He smiled and said "Hi" back.

"I am so full of energy! The night has already been so amazing," I started rambling on about everyone I had met.

"Here, hold this," he said.

He handed me a necklace with some kind of stone on the end of it. As soon as it touched my palm, my entire hand got hot.

"Wow, what is this?"

"Put it on," he gestured.

I put it around my neck. Right away the middle of my chest got really hot. I looked at him and said, "It is doing something to my heart chakra." Again those words astonished me, not knowing what I meant with saying that. He looked at me with a big smile on his face.

"It's called, Moldavite."

"It feels amazing."

I looked up into the sky and noticed a star that I had seen earlier. I looked at him and told him that I made a wish on that very star.

He looked up and said, "That is a decent star - a good one for wishing."

Then we walked to the back, where a big crowd of people were standing around the fire. After a few minutes, I went inside to get something to drink. Then, I went around the corner to the living room. A woman was standing in the living room, talking with someone. They were both looking into this glass case in the corner of the room. I peeked inside, and saw a variety of Native American artifacts. As soon as I looked at one of the artifacts, an image of a woman popped into my mind. The woman standing next to the case turned to me quickly, and very excitedly said, "You just saw my mother. I felt it, you saw her didn't you?"

I was shocked, and with hesitation said, "I guess, I am not sure."

"No, you did. Can you tell me more? What did you see?" She was getting really feisty and I did not know how to respond to her.

"It was so fast, I am not sure what just happened," I said quietly.

"You are not leaving anytime soon, are you?"

"No, I am going to be here for awhile."

She voiced, she was one of the owners of the house and introduced herself as Sandy.

"Maybe we can talk more later, and see what happens," I said.

Then, I took myself back outside. Jesse had a guitar in his hand and was singing. An empty seat was open next to him, so I sat down. As he sang I could feel myself starting to feel disoriented. I was getting dizzy, and it scared me. I got up, "You are zoning me out way too much!"

He stopped and said "Don't go," and my body seemed to sit back down.

As he sang, I thought, 'I won't go, but maybe standing would help. I am really feeling strange. I don't do drugs, but I sure feel like I am tripping out.'

I stood up and looked into the fire while he sang. Suddenly, a few of his words caught my attention. I turned around and faced him and he simply stared into my eyes as he sang. I was mesmerized with his eyes and the faint tone of his voice in the background. It seemed everything around us was disappearing again; the same experience I keep feeling with him. I closed my eyes, saying quietly to myself, "Just breathe Hope, just breathe."

For many hours of the night I was looking up to the sky trying to find the moon. I could not find it; I kept looking up but it seemed to be nowhere.

As I was looking up, I heard, "Hey, would you like to go on an adventure with me?"

I looked down and Jesse was standing right in front of me. "Sure, where are we going?"

"Come on…" he said as he started to walk towards the woods. I followed behind him as we walked towards the end of the yard. He hopped over a small wooden fence; I jumped over landing right next to him.

As we walked past an old, dark barn, he voiced, "Maybe, someone is in there watching us!"

"Is that supposed to scare me? Funny, I see ghosts all the time. I don't think an old barn is going to cut it."

We both laughed and kept walking all of a sudden I stopped right in my tracks, and could not move. I felt I should look up, and when I did, there was the moon - so bright, and so beautiful, I stood staring at it. "I love the moon. There is something about the moon; I can't explain it."

We continued to walk and found a stump to sit on next to a tree. We did not say much - simply sat side by side and stared at the sky. Then we headed back and I could see Abigail looking all around.

"Are you looking for me?" I said.

"Yes! Where have you been?"

"Jesse and I went for a walk. Found the moon!"

"Nice. I think that I may go. Is that Okay with you?"

"Are you not feeling well?" I asked with concern.

"No, I feel fine. My friend said he would give me a ride home. I can either pick up my car from your house now or in the morning. It is no problem - you only live two minutes away from me."

"Should I leave with you?"

"No, stay Hope; enjoy the rest of the night." She reassured me. "I will leave you my tent, in case you need it."

I gave her a hug, and said, "See you sometime this weekend."

I went back to the yard and started to talk with other people. I never have a problem mingling in a crowd. A few others were setting up their tents and

I saw Jesse out of the corner of my eye. He walked over to me, "Are you staying?"

"I think so."

We sat by the fire talking. He looked intensely at me and said, "Come on, you can stay with me."

His actions with his words did not feel weird; it felt right. I did not feel that anything awkward was going to occur. He had been too sweet for that to happen. Even though he had not been drinking, I had a few drinks and that worried me a little because of the past physical pain that I had experienced as a result of my drinking. I had a physically bad experience a few months prior to this that still haunted me. But being around Jesse, I couldn't fight the fact that he seemed so familiar, so comfortable.

It was getting late and the night air was cooling down. I followed him into his tent. We were laying down, and began to talk. I was wide awake. All of sudden all my insides started to vibrate; I never felt this before. I turned to him, "I think that all my chakras are going crazy right now. How I know it is my chakras is beyond me."

"Yeah," he replied.

I found myself changing the subject really quick.

"How about I tell you a story?"

"That sounds like a great plan," he answered.

I closed my eyes, and let what was coming in my mind come. Then I voiced what I was seeing, "Okay here it goes; I see a valley, and in the valley is a girl with a beautiful dress on, she is dancing in the meadow. As she turns her head she sees a castle in the distance. Her arms are straight out and she is twirling around."

As soon as I said that, I felt like I was the girl, "This is odd, the girl looked down at her bare feet in the vision, and I feel like I am looking down at my bare feet and I can feel the coolness of the grass under me. I feel like this is a past. When I have these kind of visions I can literally feel what I was seeing. This is the same feeling."

Then, as I was lost in the realization of the vision, suddenly Jesse asked, "Is she a queen?"

This startled me and I thought, 'I don't want to be a queen, I feel like I should be a servant.' Then the visual vanished and my mind started to wander...

"Jesse, one of my favorite loves stories is "Ever After" have you seen that?"

"No," he replied.

"In the movie the servant ends up with the prince. He rescues her and of course you know it has a happily ever after ending."

I laid there thinking, how strange it was. What was that? Was it a vision of the past?

"Weird. Now it is your turn to tell a story."

He started a story, about a duck named Fredo that goes to the moon. In the middle of the story, he stopped and asked me to finish the ending.

I sat quietly for a moment, 'That is so weird. I wonder if I should tell him.' My thoughts brought me back to college. I remember when I was teaching preschool that I had told everyone I was going to write some children's books. The books were going to be about a duck named Fredo who had adventured all over the world. It was odd that he brought up Fredo, and that he was a duck. That is way too much of a coincidence to deny.

So, I picked up where he left off and voiced to him what I felt the next part of the story was. Then I said to him, "Now you finish the end."

I enjoyed how we went back and forth telling the story to each other. Even though I was excited to be with Jesse, I found myself starting to doze off. But, I was fighting from falling asleep for some reason. It did not feel it was because I was with him. It felt like I was resisting something.

"I feel as if I do not want to fall asleep," I said.

He wrapped his arm around me, but I kept catching myself nodding off. I was thinking, 'Why am I afraid to fall asleep?' He continued to finish the rest of the story. I found myself staring at him. Finally, I could not keep my eyes open any longer. I awoke with a startle, and noticed Jesse sleeping. He looked so peaceful. I gazed at him while thoughts sped through my mind. I was scared he would think I was a freak for staring at him, so I closed my eyes and went back to sleep.

All of a sudden, I rolled over and found myself on top of him. 'What am I doing?'

"Why do I feel sick?" I said.

"Because I am not responding to you," he said quietly.

"Oh My God!" I scrambled off, rolled over and put my back to him. "I am so embarrassed."

I closed my eyes and thought, 'Where did that all come from? One moment I was asleep, the next moment I was on top of him.'

"I can't believe I did that."
"You are beautiful and I love you. How does that make you feel?" He said.

At that exact moment, I wanted to escape out of the tent. Instead my response to his words were, "Good, I guess." I rolled over and made myself try to go to sleep. I was actually grateful in so many ways. I was embarrassed, yet it felt good that he did not respond. As much as I wanted him to be attracted to me, it felt good that nothing happened. I have had my share of men not having any feelings, and not caring at all what happened. I was drinking and he it did not take advantage of the situation. This situation was a first for me, and I felt relief in spite of my embarrassment.

In the morning, I sat straight up. Everything that happened in the night was hitting me. I sat up, and said, "I have to go. I need to go for a run. Same old escape for me, running will ease the pain of what I am feeling."

He rubbed my back and said, "I need to tell you something. I am not sure how to even tell you."

I put my head on my knees, with my back facing him.

"I am a past life," he said.

I turned around, "You have got to be kidding me. No way! That is impossible."

"Just think though, I am here and I can help you through it," he said compassionately.

My mind was going a mile a minute, 'No way, not again! The others were so hard, and I wanted to die each time. I went into a whirl-wind with each one; it was like I was in a state of not being me. It was like I was on autopilot. I could not even express into words the pain I felt inside or physically what I went through. What is he even talking about? And how can he help me?'

"I will be here when you are done cleansing," he continued.

Still my mind was racing… 'What is he talking about - cleansing - what cleansing? What is he saying? This does not make any sense.' I sat quietly trying not to cry. My mind was still going; I could not even understand all this past life stuff. I only seemed to get tidbits of it. I remembered all the things in the past month that guidance had told me. My soul went back to that timeline, and my spirit attached itself to that person here to mend. All I kept thinking was see how crazy that sounded. I could not tell him that part, he would definitely run for the hills if I did. I was so confused; I wanted the confusion to stop.

Thoughts more thoughts, 'all I knew was, I mended my heart, and I was done. So how is it possible that there was another one? It came in loud and clear, 'You are done.' I think maybe, he does not fall into that phase of being a past life. Maybe, this past life was a good one, and had a totally different meaning.'

"You know this sleeping bag is one of the best, it is really warm!" He looked at me with a gentle smile.

Staring at him, I noticed he had a corner of the sleeping bag folded down. I crawled in, as he wrapped both his arms around me. I fell back asleep and awoke to the zipper of the tent being opened. He peeked inside the tent, and in a quiet voice said, "Hi."

He keeps melting me with these soft "Hi" motions. Every time he does that, I tingle inside. He smiled and crawled next to me. He had something in his hand, "I spent the last few hours chopping up these vegetables to make homemade soup." He grabbed the spoon, and brought it to my lips.

"You made it from scratch? Really?" Thinking how sweet that was.

"No, I am kidding, but it is really good soup."

I found myself laughing a bit, as we ate the soup. We laid back and his arm wrapped around me again. The necklace he gave me to put on started to heat up again. I could feel the middle of my chest get hot.

We both got up, and started to pack up his tent.

We were the only ones left, so we sat by the fire. He sang some more, and we talked some more. He walked by me and sat on my lap. I grabbed him and said, "Don't move, you help me stay grounded."

Again in my mind thinking, 'Grounded, what does that mean? How does he help me stay grounded - grounded to what? Whatever, I thought I am not even going to question my senses on that one. Too many new things with no understanding for me to comprehend: cleansing, grounding, and now him knowing he is a past life. How does he know about all these things?'

After a few hours, it was time to go, he had things to do. We walked to the car. After I placed my gear in the back seat, I turned to face him and gave him a hug. I took off his necklace from around my neck, and handed it to him. It felt fine to say goodbye to him.

"Wait," he said running over to his car. He handed me something, it was a light blue bracelet that said "BELEIVE" on it.

"Thanks," I said giving him a puzzled look. He seemed to know me. Did he even know that all I have been trying to do is believe? -- believe that what was happening was for real and that I was not crazy? I smiled and got in the jeep. He pulled out in front of me.

All of sudden I felt like something hit me. It was like a warm wave running through me. I started shaking badly; I was having a panic attack.

Out loud I repeated, "Come on, not again. This cannot be happening all over again!"

I could not help it; I was hysterical and pulled over on the side of the road. I put my head down on the steering wheel. I kept feeling that I had lost him again and thinking, 'should I tell him that?' It repeated over and over, I lost him again.

Then all of a sudden the vision from the night before replayed in my mind. I saw the girl twirling in the meadow; I can't do this again - the visuals of the past life were too much. Then I began to think, 'maybe, the necklace had something to do with it. Could it simple be the power in the necklace.' I was trying so hard to find a rational explanation.

I called him right away, with so much panic coming out of my voice. He was sitting silently on the other line; I started to talk to him. "I can't go through this again! I really don't think that I have the strength to get through this. For some reason I feel like I have lost you again."

"You will be Okay, try and breathe. I didn't go anywhere. I am right here." His tone was reassuring, and he was voicing his words calmly to me.

"I know, but why am I having this feeling again?"

"Can you try to focus?"

I started to feel angry. I told him I had to go. I was going for a run and that I would talk to him another time. When I hung up, I started to cry. My emotions were coming out so strong it made me want to throw up. I drove to the lake, got out with the cold air hitting me, and dragged myself to the path. I ran about half way, then turned around and went home.

I was spinning, so I took myself to lie on the bathroom floor face down. The bathroom walls were moving around me. I grabbed hold of the floor and curled up into a tight ball. The phone laying next to me began to ring. I could see it was Jesse.

"Hello," I managed to say.

"Hi, how are you feeling?"

"I am fine."

"Did you go for a run?"

"Yeah, but it was too cold, so I did not go far. I don't understand all this, why does this have to start again?"

"Hope, you are like in a cocoon right now, and
when you awaken you will be a beautiful butterfly."

"Jesse, I do not understand what happened, even   with you last night. I am embarrassed of what I may have done."

"Well, I am not attracted to you in that way," he replied.

I could feel my whole body heat up, and I wanted to cry. What way did he mean?

He continued on, "It is like when you go to the bar and…"

All of a sudden the phone went dead. My cell phone battery died and I went to find the home phone. When I finally found it, that battery was dead too.

"You have got to be kidding me, both phones?" I said to myself out loud.

I ran downstairs to take care of charging both phones. I wanted to talk to him, but knew there must be a reason both phones went dead.

'You know what - I can do this, I have gotten through this before. I had to deal with this pain with all the other past lives. In some ways it was torture, but I got through it and I am still here. I found the strength to survive then, and I will keep going with all this.'

I took myself into the bathroom and turned the water on. The edge of the tub was full of candles, and I found some music to put into the CD player. I turned the lights off and stepped into the hottest water I could tolerate - the hotter the better. I closed my eyes and sank myself into the quietness. I waited for the visuals to begin.

As I bathed in the warmth of the water it started. I could tell it was beginning, because I started to feel light headed. I took several long and slow breaths, and observed what I seeing in my mind - a Native American man. He was standing next to what looked like a fence, unmoving he seemed so peaceful and I felt like I was there with him. I observed what I was seeing, he did not move. He was smiling and staring towards me. I felt like I held my gaze with him for awhile, and then it vanished.

After about an hour, I pulled myself out of the tub and headed to bed. The phone kept ringing, but I did not feel like talking to anyone. So I placed my head on the pillow and drifted to sleep.

When I woke up I felt even worse. I went downstairs to grab my phone and noticed Jesse had left a message, "Hey, I guess we aren't allowed to talk right now. Here is my home number, call me. Just keep letting go. I love you."

What is he talking about, keep letting go - letting go of what? The foreign things he was saying to me: cleansing, letting go, grounding, attachment - what is he talking about? How can he say he loves me? He probably tells everyone he loves them. I can do this alone; I don't need his help. I should have listened to Sam, and not gotten involved. How can this feel so painful when it seemed like it was supposed to happen? When I was guided to talk to him, it came in loud and clear that we needed to connect. Wow! The drama of all this seems to go over and over. Enough is enough already!

There was something about him I couldn't explain. 'Oh well,' pushing the letters on my phone I texted him a message, "I can get through this, I have before in the past, so thanks, and good-bye."

I'll let it be. I don't ever have to see him again. Surely he will be like the others that all seemed to disappear out of my life. Before all this opened up for me, I would see the different past life men all the time; they were linked to mutual friends. Then after the recognition ran its course and I acknowledged my past ties with them, they would disappear. Jesse would probably vanish, too; he said he was a past life.

I will not run from this anymore; this pain has gone on long enough. If it was meant to be, then he will be brought in front of me or I know I will receive clear guidance on how to proceed.

I wanted to call someone, but I could not even voice what I was going through. Who could relate to such intense and intangible pain?

The feeling of autopilot and that I was a mere shell with no comprehension of anything.

I caved in and called Sam, I told her everything.

"Oh, Hope… I knew this was going to happen."

"Sam, I don't really need a lecture right now."

"I know, but…"

"No buts, Sam. It happened. I can't help that for some reason
guidance connected me with this guy."

"What about the others, though? Hope, I don't want you to have
to relive the cycle of thoughts - and I definitely don't want you to relive
the physical trauma."

"Fine, Sam. Then talk to me and let me see if I can sense anything."
I started talking about it, then something came to me, "Sam, hold on.
I am getting something." I ran upstairs and grabbed my calendar, ran
back down, and went back to the deck, "No way, Sam! I can't believe
this, I wonder if it means anything?"

"What? Hope, tell me."

"I am looking at my calendar. You know how I write everything
down, especially since all this started."

"Yeah," she said.

"There seems to be a pattern with all of them."

"What?"

"It seems like each one lasted exactly two months. I mean, I would
see them straight for a month. Then, the next month they were gone
but the obsession lasted. After I acknowledged and figured it out, then
the next one would come."

Sam started to say something, but I interrupted her, "Hold on - let
me finish - I would meet him, then two months would go by, then
a month off, then another one would start the cycle all over. Sam,
this cycle seems to be exactly on. This is weird. Don't you think it is
weird? Those months seemed so intense; I was obsessed until the next
one came into my life. Remember? Do you remember, Sam? I really
don't want to go over to much of what happened, but it is a pattern,
Sam. I had a vision with each one of them, too - and their thoughts
- Oh my goodness, Sam! I know this has to mean something!"

"Now you know," she sounded excited, "you have a month, then
you won't be obsessed with Jesse anymore."

"Whatever, Sam, it does not feel the same with him. The vision is
not similar to the others; first of all, I didn't end my life. Secondly, I

was able to voice to him all the phenomenal occurrences. And thirdly, he had the opportunity, but did not take advantage of me. Also, I am not sitting by the phone waiting for him to call. It really does feel different - I would know - I went through enough of them."

"Hope, try and stay strong. Remember you are helping people. It may not seem like that much, but look at all that you have done. I mean, who sees spirits and helps people that way? I'm sure there are people out there that do this kind of thing, but I've never heard of them. Neither one of us had even heard of chakras before. And now you are learning what they are by seeing them in people's bodies. This brings me to the other major thing with the future psychic stuff."

"Don't bring that up, Sam!"

"Why not? Are you going to hide from the fact that you are having visions? You can't hide from the fact that you are seeing things and then they are happening."

"This conversation is making me crazy!"

"That is no different than all these months, Hope."

"Thanks, I really needed to hear that!" I said sarcastically.

"Get a grip. I don't want you to get locked up and stare out a window all day drugged against your will."

"Could be easier, don't you think?"

"Funny, Hope," she said obviously not amused.

"I think that I should try and sleep all day. Just kidding…" I said then started busting out into laughter. That lightened the mood so I told Sam that I wanted to go and I would make the most out of the day, "I'll talk to you later. I am going to go write."

"Call me later, would you please?"

"Yes, Sam, I will."

Then, I felt some words come into mind. I let the words flow through my thoughts. Then I realized I was getting a poem. I grabbed my pen, and began writing. I was writing a poem and these words seem to flow on the paper:

> *She tip toes quietly through each moment of time*
> *Finding herself reliving all centuries*
> *that have aligned*
> *Bringing her to walk forward on the path*
> *of evolution and leave all behind*
> *Holding her head high and seeing the ones*

that come together
To fulfill a story shattered with time
She walks with softness
She voices with truth
She holds her heart strong to know all will come true at any given time

Hmmm… that was interesting. It sounds pretty good. I guess I will tuck away all those words. I know writing has always helped; maybe it is to keep me straight and somewhat focused.

I found myself busy all day, I took a run, and then went to the neighbors. Darleen answered the door with a smile and hello.

"Hi," I followed her through the house and to her back patio. I filled her in on everything, and she sat listening.

"Everyday for you is like a million stories in one," she voiced.

"I know. It feels that way, doesn't it?"

After hours of talking, and me sensing things, I headed home. It felt like I had not sat on my deck quietly in a long time. Staring like I use to, with a million things running through my mind, I asked myself, 'Is this what life is about, constantly analyzing each and every moment? I guess when you have so many things coming in, and you don't understand one bit then "Yes." How do you come away from doing that? There has to be a way to make this easier.'

I went inside and the clock said, 7:30. I headed upstairs and went to sleep.

When the morning came, I heard a knock on the door. I opened the door and Abigail was there smiling, "Hey, I came over to get you ready to go to the community center."

"I really am not sure if I feel up to it."

"Come on, get in the shower and get dressed. I think you should go."

"Fine, you can help yourself to anything in the kitchen; make yourself at home."

I went upstairs to get ready. I did not have the energy to spend on my appearance. I threw my hair up into a clip and put something comfortable on. We took two cars in case I wanted to leave early. We arrived late, and found two seats in the front of the room. I whispered to Abigail, "I want to leave right after. I know we usually stand around and talk. So I am just letting you know."

"Fair enough, Hope. If that is what you feel."

I was taking some notes, then all of a sudden I started to draw something. I was drawing a crescent moon, with a star to the right of it. The star had seven points to it. I was mesmerized by it and could not stop drawing it. I handed it to Abigail, with words written under the drawing, Do you know what this means?

She wrote back, "The star seems different. Perhaps power source of energy."

I have no clue what she means; I sat there and kept recreating it over and over on the paper.

The talk was good, and as always, seemed to hit right on. It was very comforting and helped in so many ways with what I was experiencing. We got ready to fold our chairs up and at that exact moment, Abigail and I both looked to the back. Jesse was standing in the back staring right at me. I seemed to lock eyes with him, and could not stop looking at him.

All of sudden I was getting something very strong. I started sensing, and was hearing what to do regarding Jesse about the past life and how to let it go.

"I know how to let it go," I said to Abigail.

"Go over to him," she said.

I walked over to him and said, "Can you meet me outside? I think I know how to let it go."

I felt excited. Maybe, this would release it - whatever this strong pull was.

He looked at me and quietly said, "Sure, I will be out in a minute."

I went out and sat quietly in my jeep, letting what I was sensing and hearing come in, *'You need to tell him you love him to let it go.'*

He approached my jeep and got in. He looked so sad, then all of sudden I could feel it. I started to cry, and then he started to cry. "I have to tell you something. I think I know how this can be let go. I have to tell you I love you, then it will let go - I guess, it means whatever needs to go will." I looked at him and voiced, "I love you." I placed my hand on his leg, but felt funny about it, so I quickly pulled it away.

I listened as he talked. He was also going through some emotional things. I wanted so much to wrap my arms around him. He seemed so sad, and I felt just as bad. I started to feel that spacey feeling as we sat in my car. It felt like I was floating, and I could not even comprehend the conversation.

After about thirty minutes, he said, "My friend is waiting. I should go."

I reached over to hug him, and he kissed me on the cheek. He opened the door and stood there staring at me in a daze, then turned to join his friend.

I grabbed the phone to call a friend of Abigail's. She told me days ago that her friend was intuitive and I should talk to her. She picked up immediately and right away voiced so many things about me and the things that were happening. I confirmed more to her the things that she was sensing. When I stopped talking, I heard the other line go silent.

"Hope, we older psychics call what is happening to you 'Barn Storming.' It is when the ability hits you hard and fast. It usually hits out of nowhere and it takes a lot out of you. I will keep you in my prayers."

Confused and scared I asked, "Is it negative? Can it harm me? How do I understand it and what am I supposed to do with it all?"

"Hope, I am sensing you will be fine. Don't try and figure it all out at once. Let the answers come to you when they are to come to you. Your gift is powerful, and I see that it is going to help many people. Keep trusting, believing, and most of all, don't give up. If you give up you will have to come back another lifetime, and do it all over again.

Who is this male energy I am seeing? I am feeling... Never mind, I will not get into all that with you." Then the phone went silent once more. She hesitated, and then voiced strongly, "I think he is your twin."

I was even more confused, and said, "I don't understand... Twin, like a brother?" I asked.

"No, and I think you will figure this out for yourself. I have to go for now, my dear. I am sure we will talk again."

I hung up the phone soaking in the conversation. It felt like we had shared so much information, but this brought even more confusion to me. Oh well, at least she seemed to have more explanations. Driving around, I finished eating the lunch I picked up and wondered if he was Okay.

I felt worried inside about him, I could feel it strong. I should call, so I did, and he picked up. As we were talking, I found that I was driving right by his place. I voiced to him, "I am close by, and would like to come talk."

"Come, I am still sitting in my car. I will wait until you get here."

I pulled into the parking lot and we walked inside together. As we were walking through the door, he said, "I need to get ready for work."

"I can leave so you can get ready."

"No, stay. I like to listen to you talk."

While he was getting dressed, he looked over at me. All of a sudden he was telling me his real name. "What?" I turned my head to look at him. This is one of those moments when I was shocked again. I was connecting information from the past to my present and it was making sense; especially when I saw the University logo t-shirt he had put on.

"Did you go there?" I asked as I pointed to his shirt.

"Yeah, I graduated this past year."

Suddenly, in a daze, I went back to a time a few years ago. I was playing the Ouija board with a friend. The board kept telling me to find my twin giving me his name and location. My friend and I thought there must be some huge family secret when that happened. Did I have a twin? I had not taken the board seriously. I am not proud of playing the board, especially with what I know about it now, and how it is not something to mess around with -- at least that is how I feel. I feel like it can open up a door to let many bad things in, unless one takes precautions. The one time my friend and I played, the palette was flying all around the board. It was spelling so many things out. It told me to find my twin, and spelled his name and where he was.

Now all of a sudden, Jesse was giving me his real name and wearing a t-shirt that spelled out the location where I was supposed to find my twin. His real name made me pause; it was the exact name the board had spelled out. The dots seemed to be connecting. The psychic clarified that Jesse might be my twin and that he was not my brother. This was too ironic; the board's premonition about a twin with a certain name…the place where I could find him…and then the psychic relaying her message to me. Now, he was standing right in front of me confirming the name and place. I was confused.

I could hear a faint sound, "Are you okay?"

I realized he was standing there, staring at me.

"Oh yeah, I am fine. It is nothing. My thoughts were someplace else is all." I explained to him what I remembered.

"I think it was me! You asked for me and I asked for you!" He voiced.

Wondering again, 'What is he talking about? You asked who?' I ignored the comment, and kept talking as he got ready for work. I started to look at some pictures on his wall and my thoughts began to fade to the background. I was looking at pictures of Jesse with short hair. Flashes of visuals I have had started coming in strong. He startled me as he came around the corner, asking, "Do you know who that is?"

"I assume it is you," as I tried to reply and focus back on him.

"Yeah, it was a little over a year ago."

I looked closer at the picture, as a white flash raced through my mind. Another ironic thing, a little over a year ago I kept having the same reoccurring vision. It was a vision of me and another man together. At that time I did not acknowledge that I was having visions. When those moments occurred I would think, 'I must have seen that in a movie.' But in this particular visual the man had short hair, and looked like Jesse did in the picture on the wall.

It was time for him to go, so we walked outside together. As we approached the parking lot, it was raining pretty hard so he stopped, "I'll give you a hug here so we don't get wet."

He hugged me, smiled, and then we both went to our cars. I stopped before I opened my door, and we stood there staring at each other. The rain did not bother me as my hair started dripping from the water. I did not want to leave that moment. I could feel his eyes as we stared at each other. I broke free from looking at him and headed home.

I called Abigail on the way back to my house. Excitedly I extended an invitation, "Hey, Abigail, I feel great! Do you want to go shopping tomorrow and spend the day together?"

"Sure, Hope, that sounds great - just come over anytime."

"I need to go now and head to work to wrap some things up." I still called it work even though I did not work there anymore. Then I started to get, 'No, don't go,' so I listened and headed home.

In the morning, on my way to Abigail's, I saw the moon. I looked up to view it. I love when I see the moon out during the day time. '*Something about the moon*,' it kept repeating over in my mind.

I walked into Abigail's, and said, "What is it with the moon?" As soon as I said it, I was getting a visual.

I collapsed on the floor and she came running over to me, "Hope, are you Okay?"

"I think so, but this visual is strong."

"Go with it," she said.

I could barely see her, but I saw her grab a piece of paper. I stayed on the floor, "Abigail, I don't think I can move."

"It is Okay, Hope. Let it come in and go with it," she sat down next to me.

I closed my eyes to relay the vision. I began to voice, "I see Jesse in the vision! Wow, Abigail, I can really feel this - it is strong!" My words began to flow out of my mouth, but I did not really comprehend what the words were. After the visual stopped flowing, I sat quietly, then began to cry, "I really don't remember much of what I said, Abigail."

I began to rub my eyes, to get a clearer view of her. The look on her face said it all. Her eyes were wide and she had a stone stare on her face.

I snapped right out of it, "What did you write?"

"Maybe we should talk about this later. Why don't we go out for the day now?"

"Wait. I remember something - it feels like a beautiful story - I can faintly feel it within me. I know if we talk about it, it will all come back to me."

"Hope, I feel that if we go into the visual again, it will really take a lot out of you. That has happened to you before, remember? After you see these things you get so tired."

"Yeah, I guess you are right. It can wait."

We walked over to her car to head out for the day. "I think I want to call him. I am so excited for some reason. I want to tell him what I saw and share it with him."

"Call him," as she smiled.

I called and he picked up. Right away I said, "Can I see you to tell you something that came to me? I would tell you right now, but I think it will come in clearer if I am with you. I really cannot remember much of it at this moment, but I feel that if I am with you it will come in stronger."

"Yeah, I want to hear about it."

"Okay, I guess when the time is right we will get together. I'll call you soon," then I hung up.

When I got home that night the vision popped in again. I could see it and feel it. Something started to happen, though - it got deeper as if I was there. It began repeating over and over and I could feel it stronger and stronger. Then my thoughts became the vision; I did not feel like I was in my room. I felt like I was in the vision - in that place of it. It was a very confusing, external feeling. I felt his presence for some reason and it seemed to hold so much love. I could feel every ounce of it. Then it seemed I was going from then to now. My thoughts seemed to feel the love, and then seemed to come back to now. My mind started to wander into what he had said. He was not attracted to me. How is that possible? How can I be seeing this visual and feeling him, and he was not attracted to me? Suddenly, all of these weird emotions started to come up. In the vision it felt so much like love. It was as if I could feel him loving me as I loved him.

I stood up, and fell against the wall. I was having a difficult time standing. I grabbed my blanket and headed to the bathroom floor again.

I was still on the bathroom floor the next day when Abigail called. Her voice came through with a tone of urgency. "I am feeling something is wrong! Are you okay?"

"I don't know. I am on the floor, and I can't seem to move my body. I am having all these confusing feelings for Jesse. I can feel his presence and attraction for me in the vision, but his words are not matching what I am seeing and feeling."

"Call him, Hope."

"No!" My voice got louder, "I don't want to talk to him. For some reason I don't - forget it. I can feel him in this vision right now, and I don't think I want to talk to him. Abigail, for some reason I am angry with him, these weird and crazy thoughts are coming in. Like, why does he not want to share this energy with me? How is this possible to meet him here, and him not respond with attraction to me? Why have I waited so long, and how does he not want to share that energy with me? I am spinning bad. I feel like I am on that ride that goes around so fast that you stick to the wall."

"Call him, Hope," she stated with a strong, firm voice, "Call him right now!"

"No."

"Then I will," she said as her voice got frantic with me.

"No. Please forget about him," I stated back to her with anger. Then I hung up. I felt bad that I had hung up on her, but I did. I wanted to hide in my blanket and not come out.

All of sudden the phone was ringing; it was Jesse, "Hey. I am coming over, Hope."

"What?"

"I am coming over right now!" He had the same urgency in his voice that Abigail did.

"No, I don't want you to. Just let me be." Then I started rambling on and on to him, "I don't even know what I am saying. How can you not be attracted to me?"

"I am very attracted to you."

"Jesse, stop - just stop - you are confusing me, and I don't know what is happening. I'm angry at you right now - and I don't understand or like being angry with you."

"Let me come over"

"No, I will get through this. I feel like I am someplace else right now. Like I am not even in my body, and it is scaring me. Yet, the place that I am seeing, feels right - I feel like I am there. So talking to you here is confusing me."

He was persistent, "How about you come over tonight? Try and take a shower. When I was going through some of this, a shower made me feel better. Why don't you put something on that makes you feel good, and then you can look nice for me, too. It might…"

"What do you mean, when you were going through some of this?" I interrupted him.

"Never mind that, why don't you come over tonight? I would love to hear about the vision you wanted to share with me."

I took a long sigh, "Fine, I will come over after dinner."

It was already late afternoon, so I dragged myself up to try and stand in the shower. I did not fully have the strength to stand up, so I sat as the water ran over my body. My body felt so weak and miserable. I could not feel relief with my emotions. Not until I would see the vision in my mind, which was filled with such love and comfort. It was like I was void of emotions; the only time I felt anything was when the vision would come to me.

I got ready, and headed towards his apartment. At this point, I did not care what happened with him. I just wanted to know what was happening to me. I called him to let him know that I was on my way.

I was so drained that it was difficult managing the drive over to his place. I began to have a vision as I drove, I was laying next to him on his bed. He was on my left side, and placed his hand on my heart chakra. I watched the vision diminish as we laid still next to each other. I returned to focus on the night, and my driving. The night felt warm, and the sky was clear.

After I parked my car, I knocked on the door and he opened it with a big smile on his face. He walked into the kitchen, and I sat in a chair next to the table. Looking over his shoulder he told me,

"I am making a salad and putting a lot of love into it."

He motioned to the cabinet opening it up,

"Oh, I want you to try something," and he grabbed what looked like a jar of peanut butter.

"It's almond butter," he said putting it on some toast and handed it to me.

Thinking, 'I am not hungry, and still was not in the mood to eat. I often would not eat for days as I went through these experiences.'

I did not want to be rude, though. He had gone to so much effort. So when he handed me the toast, I put it on the plate in front of me.

"Oh, and I want you to try something else, I made this great salad," he said extending his arm out as he handed me a bowl of it.

In some ways he was really making me laugh. He was excited and seemed so happy. He turned around the corner of the kitchen and faced me,

"Guess when my birthday is? It is in September, but do you know which day?"

"I don't know, is it the 30th?" I said, looking at him funny. I had a feeling he was asking for a reason and that it had something to do with the day. I could feel his intention. Why was he asking? I had told him the 30th because that was my Mom's birthday. I thought maybe he was sensing to ask me and linking it to her.

"No, it is the 19th," he said with a quirky grin.

"Really? Mine is on the 19th also - but a different month."

As soon as the word "month" came out of my mouth, I remembered telling Sam some time ago, that the one would have the same birthday as me; not the same month, just the same day. Faintly, I heard him say something, "What?"

"I asked for you and you asked for me," he said simply.

There he goes again, stating "I asked for you and you asked for me." I was puzzled, thinking once more, 'Who did he ask?' I did not voice that out loud, because I had no idea what he was talking about. It did make me think, 'for almost a year now, I had been asking to find the one.' No, I am sure that is not what he is talking about. Yet, he could be right in some small way - I had in the past found myself voicing out loud, "I need to find the one that will connect the missing piece to the puzzle." Surely, that could not mean the same thing. Still I was wondering if it was connected somehow.

We talked as we ate. I told him a story of how I used to do this thing with a state map. I would stand in front of the map, close my eyes, circle around and then point to some place on the map. Wherever my finger landed, I would make it a point to go there and explore the town.

"Hey, you know what? I have a map in the living room. Why don't you try it?"

So, I walked over to the map on the wall. I closed my eyes, spun around and then pointed. I pointed right to the water. He walked over to me, grabbed my shoulders and spun me around again. When I opened my eyes, he voiced, "Nice, you landed right in the Philippines. You want to go?"

"Sure, sounds good to me."

He grabbed his guitar as I took my body over to the couch. Stating to him, "You sing, I will close my eyes and take myself to the island." As he began to sing, I looked over at him, "I do seem out of it, I cannot really focus."

Looking over at me, he put his guitar down, and said, "Now I want to hear the vision."

"Are you sure?"

"Yeah, I really want to hear it."

We went into his room, and laid on his bed. He grabbed my hand, and I could feel myself going into the state of the vision. I closed my eyes to focus and began to talk, here it goes:

"Okay, I am in a place and I am sitting upright. Slightly to the right is the moon, a sphere crescent moon; reaching out, it can almost be touched. To the top right corner of the moon is a star that is so bright the corners of each can be seen, totaling seven. The middle line is longer and staring at this takes your breath away. The sky is dark black and full of small stars. I feel like I have come to this place many times to have conversations. As I am talking in the vision, I look to the right of me. The sky seems to be so pronounced and surrounds every inch of space. I am awestruck by the depths of the darkness and beauty of the faint, glimmering stars.

I see someone sitting next to me, sitting with their knees up, and back straight. Looking at each other, eyes connect, they feel almost lost and if they could disappear from everything. Talking for hours upon hours, time seems to stand still as the conversations continue. The stories they share are endless. She turns to him with the darkness behind and stars so bright, his eyes are the color of midnight blue. Everything seems to be circling. Looking into his eyes, realizing at that moment she loves him with every ounce of her heart. Saying to him, "Your love circles my heart and when it stops circling it will leave that lasting imprint that when we meet again my heart will only be able to identify. Throughout the centuries our paths will cross, but, when it is time to reconnect, all the signs will be in front of us."

Now I see them laying back. I can feel the energy coming through me. This place feels so much like home.

I turned my head to look at Jesse; I could feel energy going through my body. With a soft tone, I asked, "Can you feel it?"

"Yeah, I can."

I started to cry, I was feeling so much love, "I don't want to come back, I want to stay there with him!" Knowing and feeling the him, in the vision, was Jesse. "I remember writing that many months ago, it was my favorite thing I wrote," I paused, and then looked over into Jesse's eyes, I wrote, "Your love circles my heart and when it stops..." I could not bring myself to finish the rest. "I wrote that months and months ago!"

His eyes were staring into mine, quietly he said,

"You know what my favorite thing is?"

"What?"

"You know you are in love when you can't sleep and everything in reality feels better than it does in your dreams."

My eyes locked with his. I felt like I could not move. Then he said, "One of my favorite sayings is, "It is not about the breaths that we take in life, it's the things that take our breath away."

I turned my head and stared up to the ceiling; he had a dark cloth covered in stars that was tacked right above us.

I pointed, "Are those signs all around the edge of that?"

"Yeah, Do you know what stone that is in the middle?"

"No," looking back over at him. "But, I once had a vision wearing a ring on my finger. The ring was kind of silver but more black; I think it was black titanium. Anyways, it had all these signs engraved all around it." I did not tell him in the visual I had it on my ring finger.

"Do you see the stone in the middle? He asked, "It is a rose quartz. It means unconditional love."

I looked over at him again, in a complete spiritual delirium. Thinking, 'The signs, I felt like I was getting signs all over the place. The ring, the signs on the ceiling, even the island from the map had a strong connection in my spiritual visuals.'

This seemed to heighten the madness I was feeling inside. I was frustrated, because I was feeling I should not voice any of those things to Jesse. I did not know why, but then again, maybe it was me being scared of how he would respond.

We got up, and were heading to the door. My body atomically stopped, I turned to him. He wrapped his arms around me and held me; I felt very dizzy. He started writing something on my back.

"What are you writing on my back?" I asked.

"You are Okay," he answered.

I looked up at him. His capturing stare startled me and took my breath away. His eyes were so blue, as the midnight blue in the vision. And with the cloth hanging above, all you could see were the stars behind him.

"Wow, it is exactly like my vision," I managed to say.

He stared at me and smiled, "Maybe, it is a sign."

All of a sudden, I felt like something was circling us. I looked around us to see what it was, but was not really able to see anything. I felt in some way it was me circling us. It was me! I could feel myself circling and trying to get a good look at him. It was such a strange feeling to circle oneself - so weird, and it freaked me out. I did not say anything, but thought, 'Just let him hold me.'

As our arms wrapped around each other, we began to sway - slowly back and forth. Then I felt a sensation in body like we were falling. It felt like I was dropping out of the sky, so I held onto him tightly. All I remember is one minute seeing black, the next closing my eyes and putting my head into his chest. Trembling and leaving me to feel the sensation of dropping for hours. All of a sudden, we bounced onto the bed.

"Did you know the bed was there?" He asked.

I felt so delusional, feeling the bed and the falling sensation continue at the same time.

"I guess, I knew. It felt like we were falling, as we were dropping back. In some way I felt like you would not let anything happen to me." I answered.

We laid there silently. I was on top of him and could feel his heart pounding.

"I can feel your heartbeat."

"Yeah," he replied softly.

"Now I can feel it moving. This is weird... How is it moving?"

"Yeah, where is it now?"

"It is in the middle of your chest."

"Yeah, now where is it going?"

It was as if I could see and feel his heartbeat as it was moving towards my heart. I did not say a word; I was so entranced by what was happening. It felt absolutely beautiful.

My arms were clenched close to my body. I began to feel a soft flutter of warmth. His fingers barely caressed a portion of my back. Then as soon as I acknowledged it, something happened. I could feel all my chakras flickering. My arms released and my whole body relaxed. It felt as if a tension of pressure let free of my body and released. But, the tension was not like stress it was a beautiful experience. It was a soothing release and blissful feeling.

We scooted over to lay closer to the wall as he wrapped his arms around me and put his hand on my heart chakra. He kept his hand on my heart for awhile for awhile then wrapped it around my stomach. Exactly like I had envisioned before I arrived.

I started to rub his back, then slowly put my hand to his face. Rubbing his face, and looking at him I wanted to give him a small kiss. I resisted; a small part of me was afraid of his reaction. Everything seemed so perfect and still. No words were spoken. I felt like we did not have to say anything but enjoy the moment of holding each other.

We fell asleep. Suddenly, I woke up gasping. I jumped right up, fighting to breathe.

"Are you Okay?"

"I am fine," I laid back down on his chest and started to breathe more evenly.

In the early morning I woke up, rubbing his chest softly to wake him. His eyes slowly opened. I looked up at him and whispered, "I have to go."

"Hold on," he rose up, and asked, "Can I get you something - water, anything?"

"No, I am fine, thank you," I gave him a hug, and told him to call me. I felt great and wanted to go for a run in the woods.

I got home, showered and changed into my running gear. I got in my car. When I was halfway to the lake my phone rang. Seeing it was Abigail, I answered, "Hi. Abigail, wait. Slow down, I can barely understand you. You sound frantic. What is wrong?"

"Hope, I think that there are some spirits here. My bed is shaking and it is freaking me out. Do you see anything over here?"

"Hold on, let me zoom in," I took my mind to her room. "Yeah, you have two on each side of your bed," I could feel her fear. I turned the jeep around, and headed back towards her house, "I will be right there."

When I got over she looked white as a ghost, I sat on the bed with her, "It is fine, they feel fine. I can feel a loving presence here. I can see two standing to the left and two standing to the right."

As I watched, they formed a bright white light. The light seemed to cross over us, and form an X. I told Abigail what I was seeing.

"I think it is some kind of protection," she said and calmed down.

I told her not to be afraid and to let the fear go. Then they disappeared. When things calmed down, I told Abigail that I wanted to go for a run, but had a lot to tell her and I'd come back later.

Arriving at the lake, the center of my chest started to hurt badly. What is this pain? I was getting that it was my heart chakra. I didn't know what to do so I began to walk slowly. I picked up the pace, and began to run. As I ran, I started to feel all the energy of pain I had put around the lake.

I was getting to, *'Release it all. Let it all go.'* That makes sense; I did come to the lake almost everyday and cried as I ran. Now, I was getting to let it all go to clear the way. I came to the end of the trail, and started to feel a lot of pain. I felt that I needed to be close to the trees - and was getting, *'the pine trees are healing.'*

So I listened, found a pine tree and stood with my back against it. I could feel something lifting from me - the pain was going. I stood there for about twenty minutes and then stepped away from the tree. Wow, that was amazing. I was so pumped up. I got into my jeep and noticed a message on my phone. As I listened to the voice on the other line, it was Jesse.

"Good morning, Sunshine. It is a beautiful day. I am chilling… Give me a call."

Right away, I called him to tell him about my adventure.

"Hey! Today has been incredible," sharing all that happened with Abigail this morning and the releasing around the lake.

"That sounds incredible!"

"Yeah, it was. Oh my gosh, I wanted to tell you something else, while I was in the shower this morning I kept getting, *'my soul came back.'* All that kept coming in and repeating was that my soul came back. It is so ironic; I have been asking Abigail if she knew what it meant when your soul is in limbo. That is what had been coming to me - my soul was in limbo. Now it is back! Remember when I woke up last night? I think when I gasped for air, is when my soul came back to me. Not sure what that means, but I feel great." The other end was silent, "Are you there?"

"Yeah, I am here."

"Well, I really need to get back to Abigail's. I will call you later. Have a great day at work."

What a difference; I felt alive again. Whatever happened when I was at Jesse's, and whatever he did to help me, worked? I was no longer feeling so lost and my thoughts seemed straight and focused. I hoped it stayed that way for awhile. At least I am hearing more clearly and I got to help Abigail.

They find themselves back in the thoughts of
where they first could see
Dancing in the moon light of stars so softly
Wrapping the love of light around each moment so brace fully
To remember the heart has shown itself fully
Taking them to the softness in the sky
to just let it come to be
Bringing it to the understanding of love
has such a way
As two dance in the stars of eternity

Chapter V

THE DISTANCE BETWEEN THE TWO

*A*bigail and I sat on her couch, tea in hand. I told her all that had occurred. It was so amazing and felt so right. Every touch with him, every moment felt so beautiful.

"Sounds great - really sounds like you are in a better space," her words and expression signaled her relief.

"Abigail, I feel good. Maybe that is what needed to happen."

"I think so, too. It all sounds fascinating and incredible."

"We made plans to go run on Saturday together. I hope I can keep up with him," smiling at the thoughts of it.

"That sounds like fun."

"Yeah, I am pretty excited about it."

I was in the mood to relax so I asked, "Do you mind if I stay over tonight?"

"No, not at all. We can watch some movies and hang out!"

"I'll have to leave first thing in the morning. I am meeting with the man who voices at the community center,"

"Really? You are meeting with Joseph? That is great, Hope. He is a wise man and holds a lot of knowledge when he speaks."

"Yeah, I am being guided to meet with him."

In the morning, I woke up and got ready to go meet Joseph. I was careful to be quiet so that I would not wake Abigail. While driving, I started to feel a strong energy and the air in the car felt very heavy and thick. It almost felt like a wave of warmth. Then things kept coming to me. I sensed I needed to say to Joseph, '*Nice to see you again old friend.*' Hmm, I wonder if a spirit is trying to communicate with him. Why would I say, "Nice to see you again old friend?"

On the way, I felt a pull to go over to Jesse's. I had a little bit of time to stop by quickly before my appointment.

I knocked lightly and then went in; I knew he worked nights and I did not want to wake him. As soon as I walked in the door, I looked to my right. I noticed he was sleeping on the couch, so I went over and curled up next to him. He rolled over, and put his arm around me.

"Hi, this is an awesome surprise," he softly whispered.

"Hi, I am meeting with Joseph soon, but wanted to stop by for a moment."

As I laid with him, I started to feel like my mind was going someplace. It was like I left my body and I didn't feel present in reality at all.

I moved my head towards him, "I think I am going someplace right now." I let go and went with the visual I was having. Then I began to relay what I was seeing:

"I can see myself walking into this large room. The ceilings seem to go on and on. The room has a sort of library feel to it - not too bright, dim with a glimmer of fire-lit candles. I am seeing this amazing marble floor, and these tall candle holders. I see older looking men dressed in what looks like robes. They are at desk's writing with a unique looking pen. They seem to notice me, but are not saying anything. I can feel myself walking on the floor and I walk right past the men. Now, I am walking over to some books on a shelf - there are so many books. My hand rises to touch a book. As soon as I touch it, I see a spark fly and it shocks my hand."

Even though it was a vision, I could feel it with my physical hand. My actual hand next to Jesse began to throb, "I am now walking back towards the men writing. I am trying to look at what the men are writing, but cannot see the words. The walls are incredible; each corner seems to be lit with a tall thin candle holder. I have never seen anything like these candle holders. They seem so unique, and very beautiful. I saw myself walk around for a little bit. Now, I see myself floating back. This is how I always exit from a vision - the same way spirits exit after I communicate with them."

All of a sudden the visual was gone. I felt normal again, and looked at Jesse. He was sleeping. I whispered in his ear, "I have to go."

I felt excited, like a burst of energy was pouring through me. I gave him a kiss on the cheek, and then headed for the door. Looking at him laying there, so peaceful, I couldn't resist and went back over and gave him another kiss. I wanted to stay and cuddle with him, but I felt it was important to go. Especially since guidance had asked me to meet with Joseph.

I headed to the place we planned on meeting. I started to feel spacey again as I walked in; I did not see Joseph sitting anywhere. I looked around searching for the restroom, found it, and went straight inside. I was having a hard time breathing and standing. I looked into the mirror and my eyes started to dilate. I stood bracing myself with my hands grabbing the sink and my head down. I looked up. My eyes were still dilated and now looked red.

I walked out and spotted Joseph sitting at a table. I sat down, and started rambling. I started to cry and said, "I am so tired." Many things were coming out of my mouth. I didn't even know what I was saying. I looked at him and said, "I need to tell you, nice to see you again old friend." As soon as I said that, I began watching for the spirit that wanted the message relayed, but never saw one. I voiced to him that for some reason, if he hugged me, he would feel that person. He looked at me, nodded and smiled as he sat across from me. I told him that usually when I get a message for someone, I see a spirit, but this time was different as I was not seeing one.

He mostly sat and listened. The entire time I was hoping he did not think I was crazy. I finally said to him, "I am going fast, and I need help with my transformation."

"What do you need help with?" He asked in a slow voice.

"I don't know. I don't even know what transformation means. I have never even heard these words before."

"Hope, are you eating?"

"I am trying, but not much."

"When was the last time you ate?" saying this with concern.

"A few days ago, over at Jesse's. I feel like I know what my body weight is going down to, and that scares me."

"Please, watch it and don't go any lower than that."

He sat quietly, so I kept talking and letting the words flow out of my mouth. I started to voice to him about Jesse, and for some reason kept repeating, "Please, don't tell anyone! It seems... it is very sacred to my heart. He is sacred to me." I had no idea what I was even saying.

After about an hour and a half, he looked at me with eyes of comfort, "Hope, answer a question for me."

"Okay."

"You have not read any books about any of this stuff, have you?"

"It is funny you would ask that. I bought some books about psychics and mediums. I tried to read them but kept getting to, '*put it down*.' So I guess, the answer to that is - No, I have not read anything. So this is difficult for me, because I don't know what is happening to me. Jesse mentioned some things to me about cleansing and letting go. I have no idea what he is talking about."

"Hope, I do believe it will make sense to you as time goes by. Be strong and keep trusting. One more thing?"

"Yeah?"

"Are you sure this is what you want?"

I looked at him, and the words flew out, "To help and heal people? Yes, that is what I want." It was as if my mind did not think at all before the words came out. I always knew I wanted to help, but it was strange. When he asked if I was sure this is what I wanted, the words seemed to flowed from somewhere deep within me.

We both stood up and walked outside. He gave me a hug, and smiled.

"Hope, I will see you soon. Hang in there, and I will pray for you."

"That means a lot to me. Thank you for listening."

For some reason, I felt comfortable with him like I did Abigail and Jesse. He seemed familiar and I felt he understood. I felt like I had known him for a very long time, but I had only heard him speak a couple of times at the community center. This was the first time I had even had conversation with him. He had a soothing spirit and I felt grateful being able to talk with him.

I went home and the voices started again. I was getting so many things. Suddenly, I was hearing, '*Jesse needed to walk away.*' He needed to walk away from me? What? Why does Jesse have to walk away from me?

I called Sam, and told her what was happening,

"Why would he have to walk away from me? Maybe I am wrong. Maybe my senses are off."

"Calm down, Hope."

"But… I can feel it - it feels huge. So much has happened and so many people have been taken out of my life. You know it, Sam. I don't want him to walk away."

"You are meeting him on Saturday, so he is not walking away."

"Sam, I have to go I feel a lot of anxiety right now."

I got off the phone with Sam, and stayed in a daze all day writing. In the evening I could not sleep. I wanted to see him, so I drove over. He was not home, and I knew his door would be unlocked. He voiced to me that I could come over anytime. Even if he was not there, he told me I could go in. I went inside to write him a letter.

Feeling like I was in an old familiar pattern. Is this that obsessive feeling thing again? Oh No, No. I don't want it to be like that. I texted him to tell him I was over then took myself on the couch and fell asleep. When I awoke, I got ready to leave. He was still not home and had not replied back. I went straight home to call Sam, "Sam, please tell me no. This is not happening again."

"What happened?"

I voiced to her everything that happened during the evening.

"Hope, he probably thinks you are some nut case. You went over and took a nap at his place? What are you doing? This is not like you. You have never reacted without letting guidance come in. I know when you sense things -- you listen. Were you sensing to go over?"

"It happened so fast, I don't think I was even comprehending. I know, Sam. I see it - it is starting all over again. Why, can't it just be normal? Why do I have to feel something is taking me over? These are not my normal reactions and I know it wasn't with the other past lives either."

"Hope, sleep it off - and call me in the morning."

"All right, thanks, Sam. Love ya."

I stayed up most of the night with the television on. When I woke in the morning, I went outside. I found myself laying in the grass all morning. Completely there only in the grass absorbing the sunshine.

Then, I heard the phone ringing inside. I ran in, and looked at the caller ID. It was Jesse. I picked up and his voice sounded different.

"Oh, No, No. Something is wrong, isn't it?" I could feel my heart sinking.

"We need a vacation," he responded in a quiet voice.

"Okay, where are we going?"

"No, I can't help you with this. We need time apart."

"I knew this was coming," I found myself getting angry. I think I was getting angry because I sensed it, and because I did not want to let him go. I started to cry, "No - this is not happening. You said you could help me through this."

"I can't!" as he raised his voice.

"Jesse, this has happened so many times. People keep disappearing out of my life. Is this because of what I am going through? Tell me, do you even know? This is so messed up. Fine, whatever, I really don't care at this point anymore,"

I hung up on him. I did not like the fact that I hung up on him. I never do that and now I have done it a few times with people. I have never really fought with anyone. I am always the one that resolved matters, even the small stuff. I had never even gone to bed mad, let alone have someone mad at me. This was not right; I did not like how I was feeling.

I drove straight to Abigail's and she listened as I cried, "Hope, maybe this is supposed to happen. Maybe, this is good for both of you."

"How can this be good for both of us? He probably thinks I am crazy. Who wouldn't want to run for the hills from me? I am acting like some obsessed freak. I probably scared the crap out of him! Who could blame him? This is not normal, and I guess if I were me, I would get away from me as fast as I could. Does it ever end, Abigail?"

"Keep focusing on moving forward. Trust, please keep trusting."

"Spirits, auras, chakras... Does that really mean anything?"

"You said you wanted to help people. Now maybe, you need to go through some things first to get to that point."

As I settled down and stopped crying, I told her, "I guess I can start trying to keep my mind focused. I have been sensing and getting that I need to volunteer at a nursing home. I love to be around older people; I loved my Mom and Dad's stories. Being around older people and listening to stories may help."

"Hope, if you are sensing it, then you should. Why don't you go home and try and get quiet about it and see what comes in."

"You're right, I need to get some clarity sooner rather than later. I feel like Jesse is important. It is so strong - this feeling I have about him. What is he important for - for what? Why does it feel like he is connected to me in some strong way with all this stuff?"

"Hope, again, I feel that when the time is right, all the answers will come. You have all the answers inside of you."

"Sometimes giving up and forgetting seems like it would be easier."

"I know, try and stay strong. If you give up now, you will have to come back and do it all over again."

"What are you talking about, all over again? I keep hearing that from people. What are you guys talking about?"

"I will talk to you more about that later. Just be sure."

"Sure about what, Abigail?"

"Are you sure this is what you want?"

"You know, Abigail, Joseph just asked me the same question. Are you sure this is what you want?"

"What did you tell him?"

"Yes, this is what I want."

I went home to focus on the nursing home some more. I will wait, and when guidance comes in clearer, I will do that. That night, I started seeing things again - visions I could not explain. I saw myself doing things, like working with people in another country. In my heart, it felt so right when I visualized it and I started to question whether I was fantasizing or not. In so many of these visions, Jesse would pop into them and be standing there.

'Maybe, my mind is fantasizing. What is the difference?'

As I took a bath and closed my eyes, I was standing in a small, domed building. The floor was dirt, the walls were cracked and it looked like they were made out of mud. The people seemed foreign and I was helping a man with his arm. As I saw this I could feel it in my chest, then voiced, "Yes, this is what I want."

Day after day, the images kept coming into my mind. More and more, I found myself saying, "Yes, this is what I want." I stopped questioning whether or not it was a fantasy. I came to this conclusion, when I realized the reality of what I was seeing. I felt like the vision with the cracked walls was a clinic and I wanted to be there. I did not see fancy walls, and nice things around, and yet it felt so right. Many of our minds fantasize on bigger things, luxury things. None of my visions had any of those elements in them like a fantasy would. I started to drown myself day after day into my mind with the visions.

I did go one more time with Abigail to the community center. On that day, she picked me up and we rode together. When I got into the car she smiled and said, "How have the days been treating you?"

"Not sure, flowing with all the images I have been seeing and I have been writing a lot. I am keeping track of it all for some reason."

"I am happy to hear that, it sounds positive, Hope."

We parked, walked in, and sat in the front row. I spotted Jesse in the back. At one point, Joseph asked us all to stand. I went to stand up and my body started to fall forward. I was about to pass out, but Abigail grabbed my hand as I began to fall. I held her hand tightly and put my knee on the chair. I tried to stay focused, thinking that I didn't want to pass out here.

She leaned over, and said, "Breathe slowly."

"This feeling totally stinks and I want to leave, but I am afraid to move at this point," I whispered to her softly.

After the talk was over, I looked at her, "I am going quickly out the door." Nobody was even moving yet, but I turned to head for the exit. I looked at the door; Joseph was standing there with Jesse, staring directly at me. There was no way around him. He was standing right there.

I walked right up to Joseph and he reached over to hug me. He looked at me with concern and asked, "Are you okay?"

"I am fine, thank you." I could not even make myself look at Jesse. I hugged Joseph again and headed out the door.

I took myself right to the national park to sit in the grass. I kept getting to write. All I kept hearing was: *"Write about the visions."*

I found a spot in the sun, sat down, took my shoes off and put my feet in the grass. I grabbed my notebook and began to write. I wrote for the next two hours. Then I packed up my stuff to head home.

The days came and went. I focused mainly on the visions, adventuring when I could to Abigail's. I felt at some points, I was simply running from the fact that I knew Jesse lived in the same town.

Then one day, I started to sense him. For some reason, I could feel him. He kept popping into my mind. I felt like I needed to see him. Weeks had gone by, but it felt like years. I went over to his place, knocked and he directed me in. I looked at him, trying not to cry, "Can't we talk? I am not understanding why all this is happening like it is. Please, give me closure. If you can't do that, then say good-bye to me."

"No, and you should not be here."

"Why, Jesse?"

"You just can't."

He walked into his room, and I followed. He laid on his bed, with his arm behind his head. He looked at me and said, "Are you sure this is what you want?"

"You have got to be kidding me. You are the third one now to ask me that same question. Why does everyone keep asking me that?"

He jumped up and headed to the living room. He seemed disoriented, not happy, like he had when I saw him weeks ago. Then he said something regarding intuition, and knowing things.

My voice started to sound angry, "Would you stop with the Psychic 101 stuff already. Please, talk to me."

As he stood by his living room wall he voiced, "I can't." Pointing to the wall, he said, "I wrote this last night, as I was drinking with my friends."

I could not believe he had been drinking. I had no idea that he drank - he did not seem to cross me that way. I looked on the wall where he was pointing. It said, "You will thank me some day. Trust me." I did not say a word to him, it was all so confusing.

"You have to go," voicing to me with his head down.

"Fine. If this is how it is going to be, then I will go," I wanted to go, but it felt as though something would not let me leave.

"Please talk to me." Then my hands started to vibrate. It felt like I had little things crawling all over inside my hands. "See, what is this?" I put my hands in front of him.

"I don't know. Just go. I am not attracted to you."

My heart sank, "Why do you have to be so mean?"

I walked out the door, finding myself wanting to die and get it over with. Am I not seeing it clearly with him? In one sense I am feeling and thinking one way with him, but in the reality realm, it was different. My visuals and my reality were not matching. This is probably the most confused I have ever been with all this. He is not mean, and why would I say that? It is my perception of him, and that isn't right. It is how he feels, so who am I to judge that? It was totally wrong of me to say that to him, and now I felt horrible again. I need to escape into my bed. Wait. Better yet, go and drink it away.

So that is what I did. I went to a bar - the place I had been hanging out for over a year now when this started with the past life guys. I walked in and the owner was at the counter. I sat next to him, and ordered a strong drink. I did not have to talk about any of this, none of them knew anything. I liked it that way. Many people started coming in that I knew. I was messed up and that was a good sign for me to leave. It was late, and in no way was I able to drive under these conditions.

I called Abigail and got her out of bed. She said she could come and get me. She pulled up and I was sitting on the back deck with my head between my knees. She helped me to the car, and drove me home. The car was silent and I kept my head turned staring out the window. Pulling in the driveway, I gave her a hug and went right to bed.

Barely moving the next day, I found myself getting ready to do it all over again. I called someone that I knew from the bar, and he picked me up. My car was already there, so I needed to go get it anyways. I was in the same old pattern of being in pain. After we arrived, he said,

"Come on in, let's have a drink together."

"Why not? It seems to make everything disappear." My phone began to ring, "I will meet you inside, let me take this call."

It was Sam, "Hope, where are you?"

"I am at the bar."

"Hope, you are not. You stopped drinking."

"I know, but it helps right now, Sam."

"Don't do this to yourself again"

"No one here knows what is happening to me, Sam."

"You are only hiding, and trying to forget what happened with Jesse," she said with anger in her voice.

"So what, Sam. Who are you to judge? It is not your life being messed up, now, is it? I see freaking dead people walking around Sam. And now, I am seeing visions into who knows what and who knows where. I know things that are written in books, I am quoting prophets and knowing words of others. I'm sorry, Sam. I have got to go. I am meeting someone inside; I'll call you soon."

I went inside, and found a group of people I knew sitting at the bar. A beer was already ordered for me, and waiting. Someone yelled out, "Hey, you finally got off the phone."

After I sat down and took my first drink, I looked at Daniel next to me. "Thanks for picking me up and bringing me to get my car."

"No problem, Hope. Anything for you," he was smiling, then said, "We were all talking about something and we wanted to get your input."

"Okay, go ahead."

"The question was; how do you know if you really love someone?"

Thinking to myself, 'This is definitely not a question I need to think about right now.' But, I opened my mouth, and voiced:

"Love has so many directions and so many false starts to it too. Is it lust or is it love? Does it go beyond understanding? Does it sometimes fall into a false attraction with the ego?"

"Is that your answer?" he asked, looking at me funny.

"No, if I had to give an answer, I guess, I would say look into the eyes. The eyes will link you to the heart. The eyes are the key. You can look into someone's eyes and see into their soul. That is how you know."

"Weird answer, Hope."

"I know, but you asked. Who knows maybe love isn't even for real."

"Wow, someone does not want to talk about love."

"Can we change the subject, please? Let's talk about hockey or something."

"You are funny."

"Yeah, I use to say, I am the funniest person I know!"

"I think Hope needs a shot of liquor, everyone."

Next thing I knew, I had a shot glass in front of me. That was a weird answer. I found myself remembering something. I have never, in all my life, been able to look a man in the eyes. Funny, lately I had a few men wanting to stare at me and I would tell them to stop looking at me like that. Then of course, Jesse came into mind. The night I was over at his place, I was able to look into his eyes. I started to feel that pain thing again, and then I heard a voice.

"Hope, get out of your fog and stop thinking so much. We can always tell when you start thinking - you seem to vanish from all of us."

"I am here, for sure, I am here. See? I am listening."

"Now come on, let's dance," he grabbed my hand and we headed over to the jukebox. "This always makes you smile."

"I know. Thanks, I needed that."

Daniel was so attractive, and had always been so sweet, but I felt nothing for him. Being around him did not feel right. I felt nothing, absolutely nothing. Maybe, this is what Jesse was talking about. Maybe, there is a certain attraction and that is what he meant when he said he was not attracted to me. Yet, when I was with Jesse, I felt unexplainably drawn to him. So where does that fall into line with all of these feelings? I realized that one person could be attracted and the other may not. Then I shared the visions with him and that made being around him different. Since, I never felt I could share them with any other man. I was changing, and I could feel the difference. It seemed like my thoughts and feelings were activating differently. Images of Jesse began flashing in my mind again.

Of course, these images made me want to do another shot. Wanting to forget, I grabbed Daniel and said, "Let's go back to the bar."

We ordered another round and hung out all night. I took a cab home, and passed out.

I awoke in the morning and felt absolutely miserable. I grabbed the phone to call Abigail to help me get my jeep.

"I will be right over," she responded. "Let's go have lunch, and talk."

"Fine, I feel like I could eat a whole buffet. I am so hung over."

"You should be… Hope, what are you doing?"

"I don't know, Abigail. I guess I'm hiding like my friend, Sam, said. Did you ever lose something in life that just doesn't seem to be replaceable? Did you ever cry so hard that your eyes swelled shut? These are only things on my outside. Now, I have unexplainable things happening on the inside. I am a walking freak."

"Stop saying that, Hope."

"Well, what do I do with it? Am I helping anyone right now?"

"No, you are not. So listen clearly and you may get the answer."

The next day, I was getting it loud and clear, '*go through your closet and take out only the things you want to keep.*' What, where am I going? Then I heard, '*India.*' India? What… I was getting, '*You need to go to India for your hands.*' This was so bizarre that I had to call Abigail and tell her.

"India, huh? That sounds exciting, Hope."

"Are you kidding? I don't know a thing about it."

As soon as I said that, I started to have some visuals and expressed word for word what I was seeing. I could see streets and some statues,

"Do you think I am seeing streets in India?"

"I think so, Hope. And I wrote down every word that came out of your mouth."

"That seems to be a habit for you, Abigail. You like to write everything down. I guess it is good; I do forget sometimes what I am saying."

I then began to tell Abigail that I was sensing and hearing that I could not be around anyone for awhile. I told her that I was not sure why, but it was coming in strong.

"Ask if you can be around me?"

I got quiet within myself and I heard, '*Yes, you can.*' Then I was getting, '*write your plan.*'

"What does that mean?" I asked Abigail.

"Why don't you come over, and we can talk about it."

I headed right over and we sat in her library, "You have so many books on intuitive stuff. Have you read all these?" I asked.

"Pretty much," she answered.

"So, does some of this stuff make sense to you?"

"It does, Hope."

"Well then, what does it mean to write my plan up?"

"What do you want?" As she looked at me with a smile.

"What do you mean, what do I want? I want to help people. I want to be able to take this gift and use it in some way."

"No. I know that, Hope. What do *you* want?"

"I am not sure. What you are saying?"

"In life. How do you see it?"

"I have already told you some things that have come to me."

"I know. Now write them down, and be specific."

"Okay, I think I can do that. I am also getting to have it written by Friday, and that I need to meet with Joseph before I do. Can you call him for me and set it up?"

"Sure, I think he understands and knows the importance of all this with you."

"Abigail, I am not sure why I have to meet with Joseph before I write my plan. Then as I thought about it, I realized something. Actually you would be proud of me, instead of me voicing it was weird, I put it into another perspective. Now, I started looking at it as putting two and two together for trying to understand things. Remember the first time I met with Joseph, and I went to Jesse's first.

Well, when I got back home after my meeting, I was laying on the floor. I went back into the visual that I had at Jesse's place. The one with the men writing and all the books lined up. It kept coming to me that day that this was a place that my plan resides in. I labeled it as being the hall of records. Then after getting what I did, I remember thinking, 'Oh, maybe we wrote something up for this life time.' In the visual I saw Joseph there. Now, I am to write my plan, but have to meet Joseph first. I think this has something important to do with some kind of alignment.

After that, is when I started to see what I believe is my future. It feels like a process of some kind. Almost like steps taken in a very strict way of unfolding. I saw the hall of records; met with Joseph, then all of sudden I see future visuals. That night I was with Jesse, I believe he was the start of all this unfolding. I knew he was going to place his hand on my heart chakra. I think he may have opened it up somehow. Because, it was the very next day I met with Joseph. Then, I had all these visuals of things I want to do here to help people. Are you following this at all? Does this seem like it is making sense?"

"Hope, I think it makes perfect sense. I think that there is something to it all. I know how this works, and I know when the time is right all the answers will come to you. I think when you are ready you will know."

"Thanks Abigail, your words always help. I should go for a run, and think this through - the stuff with this plan. I'll come back in a few hours, and we can get more in detail about the plan."

"See you then."

On the way to the lake things kept coming to me. I could see visuals of book signings, a clinic and myself traveling in foreign countries -- it kept coming. What is the point to all of this, does it matter if I write it down? Is this what I am supposed to be writing down? I guess I should keep listening, and not worry if it matters.

I sat in the parking lot and sensed I should go home. Maybe, I need to be in the trees right now. But it came in loud and clear that I needed to go home, so I did.

I did not feel like thinking about the plan anymore, so I went upstairs to sit quietly. Abigail called to ask a question regarding one of her friends. She asked me if I could sense anything with her. She wanted to know if I knew why her friend was unable to get pregnant.

"I don't know. How would I know?" I replied.

"Can you try, Hope?"

"Isn't this sensing without their permission?"

"I already asked my friend, and she said it would be fine."

"Okay, let me zoom in." Recently I found myself saying that a lot. I started calling sensing for people, "zooming in." It was like I was focusing directly into seeing and sensing the person. I told her what I thought the issue was for her friend.

"Thanks, let me call you right back," she said.

I hung up and took a nap. I started to feel some pain in my back. I looked over at the corner of my room and saw a faint visual of someone standing there. I looked closer, and it looked like Jesse. It startled me. He looked like a ghost. What? How is this possible he is here? He appeared like spirits appear to me. I ignored it, and pretended I never saw it.

Abigail called me that evening and said she spoke to Joseph. I was to meet him on Thursday. It was already Tuesday, so I had one more day.

In the morning I went to the lake and sat quietly. I felt like writing what I wanted, but remembered I needed to meet with Joseph first. I wrote other things for an hour, when my body began to shake. I grabbed a chocolate bar, and ate it so fast. Chocolate, for some reason, helped when I would get shaky, or feel drained and I never kept track of how many I ate.

When I was with Darleen, she found my consuming chocolate funny. She would have a stock of chocolate bars ready whenever I came over to talk with her.

I spent the whole day at the lake, and then went to see a movie. The movies drowned the visuals and noise out. So I tried to escape into them as often as I could. I got home after dark, and my house seemed very quiet. I sank into the couch to cry. I missed the noises around here. This house use to be so full; never a quiet moment. Now, in these last few years, the only activities were spirits walking around.

I woke up with myself still on the couch. Right away I called Joseph, he asked if we could meet right then. I told him no problem, and headed to the meeting place.

The conversation was mostly about me expressing all that has happened. I voiced mostly about writing my plan. He was very supportive, and said, "Hope, sounds like things are right where they are suppose to be."

After I drove home, I focused by laying in the front yard. I grabbed a notebook to start writing the plan. I closed my eyes, and then let my hand do the rest of the work. After about an hour, I felt that I had written all that I was suppose to.

As I sat quietly, I was getting, *'Go to the beach for the weekend.'* It repeated over and over in my mind. That sounded good to me. I need to get out of here. I did not put too much thought into it, and packed a bag.

It was a habit for me to run. I had done that my entire life. When things got hard or something tragic would happen, I would pack up and go. Half the time, I would drive and end up in someplace unknown. I guess, it was long overdue to escape somewhere else; I threw my bag and groceries in the jeep and left.

I called Abigail, and told her I was leaving for a few days. She started to question me, and I told her I was sensing to go.

"I will talk to you in a few days, I need to get out of here," I told her, and then we agreed to talk later.

My friend back home had a place at the beach, and I was only two hours away from it. She lived back in my hometown where I grew up. We had been friends since we were fifteen.

Her condo was always vacant this time of year, and I knew where the keys were. I called her to make sure I could stay for the weekend. She said it was no problem, and to call her when I got there.

After arriving, I went down to feel the warmth of the sand under my feet. I started to write. I filled three pages, closed the notebook and went inside. I did not plan on leaving the condo which was why I brought everything I would need with me. I unpacked and opened up some of my notebooks. So many writings and words; I had written all my experiences down. One after another - there were so many. I looked at what I wrote on the beach and it was odd. I had written at length about releasing myself and letting go of the old me. I seemed to have written it more than once. I spent three days writing and voicing. I kept voicing that I was letting go.

As I was writing I heard some sounds coming from outside. A bunch of men were drinking and having a good time. I went out onto the balcony; they looked up at me and waved at me to join them. The temptation was there, but then I resisted and stood observing them as they fell all over the place. That was not what I wanted anymore. I realized I didn't want to get sucked back into that pattern again. I was hearing in my mind loud and clear, *'no more, that was over.'* I went back inside and let myself fall asleep.

After three days, I headed back home, and went straight to Abigail's. I walked around to the backdoor to make sure she was not working, and then let myself into the house. She was sitting at the kitchen table, and looked up at me with a smile,

"So how do you feel?"

"I feel pretty good, really tired though."

"Good, let's eat something."

She was always trying to feed me, but I guess that was good, since I was having a hard time eating. Her voice quieted, and she asked, "Are you still in some isolation?"

"I guess so. I am still getting it loud and clear not to be around anyone - stay to myself for awhile. I don't think I want to even question it anymore."

"Good, don't question - let it be."

"Abigail, I really don't feel well. I am going home, and will call you later."

"Wait. I want to help, if I can."

"Well, if you want to help, then see if you can sense anything. Abigail, this is hard, and I cannot explain what I am feeling. I feel like I want to rip my skin off, and that some light is going to explode inside of me. It is tripping me out, I keep getting that some light is going to explode inside of me. Can you explain why my body is feeling like this?"

"Hope, maybe things will come to you, if we talk. I only have a few minutes because I have a photo shoot soon, but can talk until then. If you want, come over in a few hours."

"That sounds good, Abigail, but I have to make a call tonight. My friend Sam has a friend that needs help. This woman lost two of her children in a car accident. I think I saw the children in their rooms in the house, so the woman wants to talk to me. I don't know it seems after I have done things like this, I get into a depressed state. Remember how I gave that reading to Tim a few weeks ago - the guy from the community center?"

She had gone with me, so she remembered right away. "Yeah, what about it? It was amazing, Hope. You read three spirits that night."

"I know. It helped and gave him so much clarity for his path. After, remember I fell into that depression state? I feel so on when I am doing the work, but when it is done I don't feel that connection - that spark. The contrast is unbearable and even though I am getting stronger with things, I still find myself longing for him - especially right after a reading. It is like I disconnect, then all of a sudden start to miss Jesse."

"Hope, can you zoom in and see if you can get why."

So I focused, "I don't know Abigail it is not clear. I miss Jesse after I am done; my mind jumps right into the thoughts with him. Then I get really sad, and cannot even explain why - the sadness it seems to overtake me. I am fine during the session, but when it's over, he pops into mind. Then there is this other thing that I was going to completely keep to myself…"

"You can share it with me if you wish. I will keep it safe with me."

"I have seen Jesse's spirit around me, and let me tell you, it is freaking me out. How is that one even possible? If he is still here on Earth, then how can I be seeing him? What if it is something bad? I know that there are negative spirits out there. What if it is something negative and I just think it looks like Jesse?"

"Honestly, Hope, I don't think it is bad. Does it feel bad? You know Jesse's energy, does it feel like him?"

"Yeah, I can actually feel his presence, like I do when I am with him. It is really peaceful."

"Hope, I think maybe you should call him."

"What? Are you serious? No way."

"Call him, and tell him that his higher self has been visiting you. Hope, I think he will understand; he is very aware. Tell him to release you."

"What?! Release me? That is crazy. He will think I am crazy."

"Do it. Call him; I think you should tell him."

"Fine." I picked up the phone, dialed his number and left him a message. I really trusted Abigail where I did not seem to trust many others with this stuff. I felt a very strong trust with her and she had already proven to be a good friend. We sat for a few more minutes when the phone rang - it was him.

I walked outside trying to figure out a way to voice what I needed to. I told him about the light bursting in my body. He jumped in and said, "I have been waiting along time for this call."

"What, anyways I need you to let me go, whatever that means." He seemed to understand what I was saying, and said, "I release you."

Then, I told him I had an important call that evening, and that I didn't want to be distracted anymore. I wanted to stay focused. The longer we talked, I found myself not even knowing what I was saying. This was so common when I was around him. I would get lost into my words, like I was speaking from someplace else. It was obvious from some of his words that he did not want to be with me. I calmed down the more I spoke with him, but his words made me want to cry. I could not take the non-matching of reality any more as it contrasted with my visions. I started to feel weird again so I wanted to get out of there.

As I left Abigail's for home, I continued to talk with him. All of a sudden it felt like my whole body was spinning. "I can't do this anymore, I want it to be over," I told him.

"If you give up now, you will have to come back and do it all over again," he said.

"What?! I am not doing this all over again, and you are the second person that has said that to me. I don't even know if I believe in that. It would be easier to check out now, than worry if you are right. I have to go."

I got off the phone with him, and pulled into my driveway. Sitting and thinking, 'Was this it? I can't take it anymore. I can't do this any longer, something is wrong with me. No one understands - I feel all this pressure in my body. It feels like my heartbeat is racing, and that I was going to explode. I can't even stand the clothes on my body. I want to rip them off.'

I ran upstairs to the bathroom, pulling all the drawers out and pushed through them searching for something - anything to take away the pain. My mind was not in a good space; I wanted something in the drawer to help me end all this.   I found a razor blade, and sat on the floor. I had the blade in my hand and was about to cut my wrist! Logically I could not think straight. It never entered or crossed my mind that it might not be Okay to end my life. I felt sadness, I felt loss, and I did not want to be here any longer. As the blade hit my arm and a small cut started to form on my wrist, the phone started to ring.

It startled me - the phone was next to me on the bathroom floor. For some odd reason it was there, I didn't remember leaving it there. I looked over at the caller ID. It was Abigail so I grabbed it and she was screaming into the phone, she was hysterical. I could not make out what she was saying. Then, in a loud voice I could hear her say clearly,

"I did not even know you left. Promise me you won't do anything until I get there! Hope, say those words, say: I promise I won't do anything until you get here."

"Fine, I promise."

"Good, I will be there in two minutes," I hung up the phone, and was in shock. How did she know? Then I started to cry, and wondered how that was even possible? Did she know I was holding a razor blade in my hand? This was so weird. I had never even heard her raise her voice before.

I jumped in the shower and threw my robe on. She came running into the bathroom, and grabbed the blade off the counter. We went downstairs and she made some tea. We sat on the couch, and she hugged me tight as I cried.

"Abigail, what is happening?"

"Hope, people on this path take certain steps. Many go up the steps one at a time, you have gone from step one to step twenty. You are just going faster than most, and I don't really know why."

"Why, do I feel this pull with Jesse? It feels like I have known him for a very long time, and feels like we should be together. It feels like something is missing. I feel and see one thing in my mind with visuals, and then being here now does not match. All those visions I have had, the ones with what I think are future. He is in them, and I have tried to take him out, but he pops right back. I feel a different kind of love with him, and it doesn't feel like my normal way of loving someone."

"It will be fine, I promise. Try and put it outside of yourself for right now. Or, can you imagine Jesse then place him in your heart. Do not let the thoughts of him distract you right now."

"Abigail, remember when we were sitting in your car a few weeks ago, and I started to zone out? Remember what I was saying about one of us had to go?"

"Yeah, I remember you were crying and said that one of you had to go. You kept voicing you did not want him to go, and that you would go."

"Yeah, and we had no idea what that meant. Now he is leaving for the mountains!"

"I know, Hope. I heard. I also, heard he was leaving for along time."

"What? How long? I don't want him to leave for a long time."

"It is good, Hope. For whatever reason you need to focus right now and not think about what he is doing. Let it go."

"I can't help it, I can feel him, and now I seem to be seeing him. All this is such insanity."

"Stop saying that! I don't want you to use any of those words again. No more words like crazy, insanity, weird - nothing. You are not crazy, and it will make sense some day."

"Can you stay tonight, Abigail? I could use the support right now."

"Yeah, let me run home and get some clothes. I have to take care of a few things. I left right when I was in the middle of a photo shoot, so I need to make sure it went well. I left my assistant to take care of it so I could run over here."

She left, and I started to feel better, but my mind was still racing. He would not leave my mind.

As soon as she came back, I started to see some things. Many spirits started to fill up my living room. I started to tell her what I was seeing. They seemed to be familiar spirits. Then I saw a light and it looked like a tunnel. I could see myself with the spirits, and I could see myself going into the tunnel. I went with what I was experiencing, and Abigail wrote it down.

After I came out of all I was seeing, she stood still staring at me,

"That was beautiful and amazing, Hope. How do you feel?"

"I feel like it is some kind of goodbye, but I'm not sure. It did seem strange, and the contents of it felt delusional. Many of the spirits I saw were ones I have already seen - mostly ones that I have the visions with - the ones that came and placed protection around me over the last year. Remember some of the stories that I shared with you about how they surrounded me and placed protection upon me.

During this time, I met this older man who walked years with a traveling master. He helped me a lot with understanding things. He was a very nice man, and did much traveling throughout the East. A very spiritual man who had a peaceful way about him. I met him at the institute that Darleen and I went to. He was fascinated to hear all these things were coming to me without meditation.

He invited me over one time, and the whole day he wanted to hear my stories. I enjoyed it, he was quite interesting. His house was fascinating with so much from all over the world. Anyways, after that I would talk with him on the phone quite a bit. He is the one I shared the visuals with, and would tell me that it was a protection thing being placed around me. Old souls came, wise ones, Native American

Indians, etc. I could go on and on. I was grateful that I met him. He did share some things with me, with all of his understanding. It did help. He is the one that helped me realize I was getting all the protection put around me from the spirits."

"See Hope, you have met others to help you along the way. So now, trust that it will still keep happening. Trust that if you keep going, ones will come and help."

"Thanks Abigail. I wish I could believe being in such a fog all the time will make sense someday. I feel like I am spaced out all the time. Floating so high up that I can't get down. I do pray ones will cross my path, when the help is needed."

The next day Abigail got ready to go to the community center, "Would you like to come with me?" She asked.

I asked myself, and told her, "I am sensing and getting, '*No, you should not go.*'

I seemed fine, so she left. I was so tired, and could barely move. It was not hard to sleep that day, so I did. I slept all day, and into the night.

The next morning I woke up in so much pain. I was sweating so bad that I was soaking wet. I grabbed the phone and called Abigail. The pain was so intense and coming from my spine. She picked up the phone and I was hysterical telling her about the pain.

"Hope, Hope, just breathe!" she said, trying to calm me down.

"Abigail, I am in so much pain, and I am sweating so bad. The strange thing is the smell. Abigail, the smell - it smells like burning flesh. I can't even breathe, and my spine feels like it is crushing."

"Take a deep breath, Hope. If you can, go get a gallon of water. Please, get the water, and try and lay down. Ask if I can come over."

"I am getting a loud, '*NO.*' I have never experienced pain so bad like this. Abigail, I can barely walk."

"Lay down if you can. Breathe slowly, and try to sleep as much as you can. Remember this, that no matter what you see, that you are beautiful and that I love you. You will be fine, I promise you."

"Are you going to give me any explanation?"

"Hope, I cannot give you any explanation. Please, keep trusting. I feel this is some type of cleansing. It seems you are releasing a lot of toxins in your body."

"Great! How long does that go on for?"

"I am not sure, try to stay strong and positive."

I hung up the phone, and refused to panic too much. The smell - Dear God - what is that smell? I found myself on my knees, with my arms over the bed. Not moving, barely breathing, and voicing out loud that I needed some help.

At that moment, I started sensing things. I could hear a voice telling me, *follow your breath.* I climbed into bed, and laid there naked.

I looked over across my room and saw the silhouette of Jesse standing there. As I stared at him, I could feel some comfort in me. It felt peaceful, and was helping with the pain. I watched as he came closer, and then laid next to me. It was so odd, and I think it would have freaked most people out. Here I was seeing spirits for other people to help them. Now I am seeing a spirit of someone I barely know laying right next to me. I let the seeing with wonder of it go and tried to absorb the feeling.

Having his spirit around was helping with the pain, how I did not know, but I could feel it. I was on my side, and could feel him holding me. I could even feel a heart beat on my back. At this point I did not care what I was seeing. All I knew was, whatever it was, it helped me relax. I could feel love, and this helped with the pain. So I did not try and analyze it - I wanted the pain to go away. It was as if he was holding me, I could feel his energy. When I acknowledged this, everything else went away.

I let the moments of pain come piercing through my body, which brought bolts of heat attacking through my spine. It would twist and turn, making my body jump as I screamed each time. I was sweating so badly, that my sheets were soaking wet.

I stared at the walls and tried to focus on what guidance I could. I was told to visualize people that I loved. As I did that I saw them standing in a line.

Then I was guided to look each person into the eyes. It was like a lineup, and I would see myself there, looking each person in the eyes then moving to the next person. Each time I would look into the eyes of someone, I felt some relief in my body.

This was an exercise I did over and over, battling with the pain in-between.

I would get glimpses of Jesse next to me on the bed. This brought ease, and was helping me to start setting a calmness of love within myself.

So, I listened intently for the entire day. I did not let the creepy things I was seeing bother me. I was seeing some pretty horrible visuals, but I trusted that Abigail knew what she was saying. I was trying not to panic. I knew I would get through this.

Abigail called me in the evening, "How are you?"

"I am fine," crying as I told her, "I am letting it happen, whatever that may be. I have tried to take a bath, for the pain and the smell. They are both still there. You should smell my arms; it is coming right out of my skin. I smell like I am on fire, my whole body."

"It will pass, Hope."

"Abigail, how do you explain something like this and not get locked up? I cannot believe this is an illusion of something I am making up or hallucinating. People often say an illusion is something we make up. I feel this illusion is real. It is so real, and I am experiencing each second and each moment of it - mentally, physically, and with my sight also. Is this how a visionary sees? Do all visionaries experience this? Is this because I am a visionary?"

"Hope, seriously, let the experience come. Maybe this is happening for you to help others in the future."

Exhausted and uninspired, I said, "Abigail, I don't really feel like talking anymore, my energy is low."

"Please, call me if I can help."

I said good-bye and took myself back to my bed. All I remembered was Jesse, and at one point the different people coming into mind. I was told still to keep looking at them - into their eyes - keep looking at the visions of them and into their eyes. It helped, and I found myself up most of the evening. I could not eat anything part of me wanted to, but I did not have the strength to go downstairs.

The next day, although I still smelled like burning flesh, the back pain was not as intense. I called Sam since I hadn't spoken with her since this pain started.

"Hi Sam, I have so much to tell you. But first, if I try and sense things would you write it down?"

"Sure Hope, go ahead. Is everything alright?"

"Yeah, I think it will be. I need to try and sense right now."

So that is what we did. I was hearing that I needed to go to India and that I still could not be around anyone. The only person I could now be around was Abigail, but I was not getting the reason why she was the only one.

"That was pretty intense, Hope."

"I guess I should trust it, and I know things will eventually make sense."

For the next hour I explained to Sam all that had occurred with the pain. "Sam, while I was laying in bed yesterday and all this was happening, I started to remember something. Do you remember when all this started and songs would come to me? It seemed that songs would talk to me and give me messages. Guidance would tell me to listen to the words, and then it seemed to match what was happening to me."

"Yeah, I remember. Didn't you get four specific ones and you had to buy the CD's?"

"Yeah, and each song was number seven on that CD. It seemed to hold a pattern, and I watched the pattern carefully. Even with music right now, I seem to escape into it. It helps, and I have found when I lay in the bathroom or when I am in my car I can't hear it loud enough. Funny thing, too - as I am screaming the words and singing as loud as I can - it helps. I had the radio on while this was happening and the songs that came on made me smile. First I heard, "One love, one heart, let's get together and be alright." Then I heard, "I am leaving on a jet plane, don't know when I'll be back again. Do you know those songs?

"Yeah, I am familiar with both of them. Seems like more messages."

"That is what you would think! The irony of all this and then the music coming in to give messages of comfort. So I think that this entire time, from the beginning, I was getting many signs and messages."

"So, how do you smell now?"

"Funny, Sam. I still stink, thank you very much."

"I hope you are sensing to write all of this down. Hope, you really should."

"I am. I let all the things come in, poems and all. I guess I thought to soon that yesterday was all of it. I am starting to get pains bad again,

Sam. I may need a few days to get through this. I will talk to you when I can. I am getting really tired again."

"Hang in there, you will be fine and I will talk to you soon."

The few days turned into months. It dragged on like this, with me alone, except for my contact with Abigail. She seemed to be the only one that could touch me, and again I did not have any reason for this. The pain would come in my back, and she would rub it out. I kept hearing, loud and clear, that no one else should touch my back. Each day and each moment, she seemed to understand and this relieved me. I was still seeing Jesse around me - time with his spirit became a part of my days. Sam understood, and told me to contact her when I could.

On days I was guided to meet with Joseph, a time to meet him would come to me. I would voice it, and he would make the time to meet with me. He was honoring when guidance would come in for me to have contact with him.

One particular day, I headed to the same coffee shop we met the first time. I felt so paranoid. I did not feel like I belonged in that environment, and was nervously looking around. Joseph asked me if I was alright. I looked at him and said, "Yes. I think I am, but I don't know what to make about seeing Jesse around me all the time." He looked at me and with a small smile said,

"Feels like a little piece of heaven."

It lit me right up, "Yeah, it does. That is exactly how it feels. It is strange, but when I see him, then I have visions with him in them. It feels so right, and love seems to pour through me. I can't really explain it; it feels like my own illusion. With such an illusion of love that does not even exist here."

We sat and talked for a good hour, and he was very supportive. I did not tell him about the spine pain. We mainly talked about the visions. I told him that I was doing some work with Abigail - with some issues she had - mostly zooming in on things, and working with that.

His words were so encouraging, but I was feeling how much he didn't know - how much I hadn't told him. Did he truly know what was happening to me? I knew and felt that for some reason. We had a similar level and some depth of spiritual understanding that was beyond me - a connection. I would be told to meet with him, voice my experiences and then things would happen. I felt like Joseph was linked to me in some way, but I was too tired to even go on about it. I simply absorbed the conversation and listened. This helped and seemed to be what mattered the most. We parted with a hug and a, "see you soon."

For three months I experienced what I called, isolation time. I was being guided to go through things - and felt I was leaving soon. When the three months was over, I finally sensed that I could be around people again.

I got ready and went straight over to Darleen's. I shared everything with her that had happened during those months of solitude and told her that I was getting that I needed to go to the community center that evening. We talked, but I felt different around her. I could not stay long. We did not seem to connect as much during the conversation. What was unfolding seemed deeper than either one of us could understand. I felt like more confusion came from the conversation, than encouragement.

It made me think about how grateful I had been to have her in my life when all this was happening. She was truly an important part and played a big supportive role for me.

I left and went back to the house to get ready to go. I headed to the community center, and when I got there I started to feel unbearably sick. I made it into the building and was guided to tell Joseph something - I was to tell him, '*It is almost time.*' I went up to him, relayed the message and walked away. I was frustrated and wondered what it all meant; I was not getting anything. I had been guided to tell him different little things like that before. I never understood why, or what it meant. The exhaustion was taking me over; I was so tired of thinking and voicing, "What does it mean?"

I headed outside, and literally felt like I could not drive away. I called Abigail, "I can't seem to leave the parking lot."

"Where do you see yourself?" she asked.

I closed my eyes and told her, "I see myself in your spare room for some reason."

"Why don't you come stay the night then?"

"Okay, I wanted to get my things first." But I was getting, '*No, go straight over.*'

I listened and headed over. Abigail opened the door and led me down the hallway.

"I am really feeling out of it."

"Maybe you should try and rest," she said and held her hand out toward the bed.

I went right into the room; there was a twin bed against the wall. I laid on the bed, and started to see something.

"Hope, maybe it would be best if we talk in the morning," she turned, closing the door behind her.

I felt very strange. I closed my eyes and could see a bright room. In the room, were all these people and I could see myself sitting in a chair. A male figure sat in front of me, staring. I could see myself slipping off the chair and sliding down. He raised his hands and said, "Come back to us, Hope. Up, up, come up."

This went on for an hour or so, then finally I was stable in the chair. Once that happened, I could see him in detail, and he spoke clearly to me. It was like having a conversation with someone right in front of me. He voiced words to me, and I listened. Then, I felt myself fading.

I rolled over in the bed, and grabbed my notebook and pen. I tried to remember all the words that were spoken. I wrote, and it seemed that I was writing about things I was going to learn in the future. I do remember getting, '*You will learn from them.*' This was where it all began with learning from the ones I call, 'My Elders.'

The next morning I woke up and headed to the kitchen. Abigail made me breakfast, but I couldn't eat - I sat tossing my eggs from side to side on my plate. I told her what I saw, and what I had written.

"I think that this is exciting, Hope. It sounds like they may be teachers for you."

"Maybe, it was pretty powerful. Oh, they did say something else. They kept repeating, '*Circle Of Empowerment,*' and they seemed to be sitting in a circle around me. They voiced, '*Your power is of our power.*'

"Weird, huh?"

"There you go again saying weird."

"Sorry, I am working on that. It is hard not to think it is weird. I keep thinking even if I were an unstable person, I could not even make this stuff up. It seems too far fetched for that to even be possible. Who knows? Maybe this will help me understand all of this. I remember feeling very peaceful - even when the visual ended. That felt really good, and it was so strong and clear - a different level of clarity. I am going to take care of some things at the house and I will call you when I am done." I gave her a hug, and then drove home.

As soon as I pulled into the drive way, I felt a strong sense of sadness. I walked through the garage, into the side door. As soon as I entered the house I felt like I had walked into a sauna. It was not heat, but the air was so thick. It was suffocating, and I could barely breathe. I walked up the stairs, and as soon as I reached the bedroom, I thought I was going to need an oxygen mask. I could barely catch my breath. I sat on the chair in my room. "What is going on?" Then I got it, "No way, you have got to be kidding me." I started to cry, and grabbed the phone to call Abigail.
    "I sensed you were going to call."
    "What is this now?" Crying, I then asked, "Abigail, why am I getting, 'You have to leave'? Why, am I getting, 'The energy has shifted in your home'? I am getting, 'You have to leave. It is time to go. You have to go to Abigail's house,' and 'take only your clothes!' Abigail, tell me I am wrong! Tell me that what I am getting is wrong! I know this has to be wrong."
    "Hope, if the Universe told you to leave, would you?"
    "Of course not," I said, hysterically.
    "Exactly. You would not move on."
    "No, I would not have moved. This does not seem fair. Abigail, I literally cannot even take a breath in here. Were you already sensing this, did you know?" I asked her, feeling like she could have at least warned me.
    "Come when you are ready."
    "Well, I guess that has to be soon, doesn't it. I can't breathe. I can't stop crying and I feel very angry." I grabbed the bag I had already packed, and threw it into the jeep. Then, I thought, 'Maybe if I sit outside on the deck for awhile, I can go back inside and be able to breathe.' I sat outside for a couple of hours, staring at the trees.
    Then I went back inside, bending over trying to grasp for a breath. This was so unfair. I grabbed a few plastic tubs and filled them with clothes. I went to grab a pillow and was getting a loud, 'NO.' I threw

the pillow across the room. "I can't even take my pillows? What is this all about? Should I even listen? This is so… so crazy."

I was stomping all over the place, having a tantrum like a small child. I was already at such a strong place of listening to guidance, that it was loud and clear. It was hard to justify to myself that, and even when I tried to grab a pillow it would get louder and louder in my head, '*NO.*'

I found myself arguing with myself and then would resign to the guidance. Yelling, "Fine, I am listening."

I put the tubs in the jeep and drove over to Abigail's. We went into the small room that I had stayed in the night before. Some changes had been made: the closet was empty, the shelves on the wall were empty and the desk against the wall was cleared.

"You can do some of your writings here if you like," as she pointed to the desk. She had placed some beautiful fresh cut flowers on the nightstand. I sat on the bed and cried, "You knew - didn't you?"

She sat next to me and hugged me, "Yeah, I was getting you were coming. I just couldn't tell you. You had to figure it out for yourself. It will be fine, Hope. You will be fine, I promise. You can stay as long as you have to and need to. Don't worry about anything. I am sure it will all be taken care of."

"Do you mind if I sleep for a bit? I am suddenly feeling very tired."

"Not at all. I will see you later, when you are ready to talk," then she turned and walked towards the door.

"Hey… Thank you, Abigail."

Smiling, she closed the door. I laid back, really feeling like I was in a daze. What is happening was I not being grateful that she was letting me stay? Then again, I had a home. This was so confusing. What would happen next? Where is this leading me? What road is this taking me down?

Each passing moment that goes by
Each whisper I hear in the sky
Each flicker of sun that shimmers in my eyes
Each motion that glides on by
Each hope that perceives and dances with glee
Each drop of beauty from within the trees
Each silence and wonder what will be
Each stream that runs so freely
This will always be the many essence of me
for all to see

Chapter VI

FLIP SIDE OF THOUGHTS

*F*inding the road has led me to where I reside right now, with a pen in my hand and a stack of papers surrounding me. The pen slowly glided as the words followed, "Where is this leading me? What road is this taking me down?"

I dropped the pen, as I could feel a pain in my stomach area. I raised my head to look out the window. Then I looked back down and observed all that I had written. Most everything that I have ever written and experienced is in that small stack of papers sitting right next to me - words guided to get down on paper, for a purpose simply to be heard.

I walked to the window and looked out at the mass of tall buildings. Turning around and facing the small space that I was in. I was surrounded with this very moment of where I stood right now.

I have come so far from what was then, to what is now. My reality of now, is to watch so much unfold and happen.

My storyline is filled with so many years, but what is constructed on these pages consist of only a year or so. It seemed to just be a bleep, divided with time. A mere representation of glimpses that led me on this adventure from leaving Abigail's to right now. That last statement, those last happenings were almost two years ago.

I proclaimed finally within myself, "Now, the I that symbolized the name, Hope, seems to transfer in my mind as she; leaving each one of these symbols as a figment, labeled, of what we think we are supposed to be."

In the beginning of the story, "I" was stated to form the acknowledgment of my name being Hope.

Now, Hope transforms back into the she, as it was written in the beginning.

All three elements - I, Hope, She - is really the completion of who "I am."

Meaning, one person here to find the truth of the "I am."

As I think of this further, I do feel that the illusion is the she part of me. The illusion of my own thoughts; she does hold such a love for him - a love that is placed in an illusion of someplace else.

Therefore, bringing that love from that illusion to show me all the love within me. It is a love, "I" found I have had all along. A love I share from the heart for what I do, and to bring out for others to experience and feel. I do remember the feelings as I went on with what happened to me.

I sat back on the rug and leaned against the couch. I looked over once more to see the stack of papers and pen sitting silently. I closed my eyes to replay through what was experienced with all the memories.

What memories I experienced, as if my mind was now the observer, of the she, I, Hope, seemed to flow forward.

The observer that was to remember what occurred with Jesse, and how he seemed to be him in my thoughts. I sat quietly with my imagination and mind.

I remembered the importance and my view; the true aspect of my illusion of the love story. As I explained the experiences of reality with the moments and glimpses of being with him, I had the true moments of touching the 'one' in my reality, as our paths crossed. The one that held the illusion at that time period, which I found was necessary for my growth. The intertwining brought much of the path that unfolded in and out of my story that continues from the journey that took me to Abigail's.

After I moved in with Abigail, I went through what I called a major part of my transformation. I stayed with her for three months, and in that time processed much of my awareness. While undertaking this source of awareness, I went through more painful experiences. I did have moments that I will never forget, as she cared for me. To this day, when I think of her, I find myself blessing her heart for all that she did.

I had times where I could not even move or feed myself. Abigail took the time to care for me, as each day for me was curled up on the floor in tears.

The days were filled with her helping me to the bathroom, and walking me to the garden to sit. Sometimes I was not even capable of standing on my own, so I would stay in bed. At the same time, I would not be able to sleep and spent many sleepless nights wondering when this would end. During the days, surges of heat would run up and down my spine, bringing me back to the floor.

She was there every step of the way. The times in between her caring for me I would have conversations with my mentors. I had three very powerful men in my life during this time. These were very spiritual men that I honored and their encouraging words of hope kept me going. My senses did get stronger, and everyday I worked with learning and trying to understand.

The Elders did channel in quite a bit, I would see myself in the same place with the chair. I say "channel" in the effect that I would get the information - the words. I started calling this channeling awhile ago, which now made more sense to me. It was like a wave of thoughts or words coming from them to me. I would see myself in front of them, and could hear clearly what they were saying. I found what they taught me was written in other books. I honored what I was seeing, and listened closely to what I was hearing. I learned stomach breathing, mind control and different meditations from them. When the Elders were not teaching me, I was getting different visuals of bodily movements in my mind. The moves would come to me and I would practice them in my room. I later discovered I was doing Tai Chi and yoga. It felt good to be able to bring the visual into my reality.

During my time with Abigail I was guided to give everything up, including all my possessions and even my money. I closed my accounts, and followed the unknown path of guidance. I was listening to the blindness of existence, letting it guide me and direct me to those in of need of help.

I felt I was bringing that one ounce of hope they held within themselves. This seemed to me like a buried treasure... the one ounce of hope - the I am - the all within you. I trusted that this was the right thing. I trusted and my faith grew stronger to believe more in my guidance. I watched the process prove itself more and more each step of the way.

Then there was the faith and trust with Jesse. I had two different accounts where I ran into him. I remember them so clearly, and remember how seeing him confused me. I saw and felt different things in my illusion mind, again the reality was not matching that.

A short hello as I passed him, a small stare with a smile. Abigail would talk to me about him and I would lay there and listen intently to what she had to say. I did ask her one time, "Why, do you keep him alive for me? Why, can I not see in reality or think that I need to let him go? Why, can we not say it is not meant to be, and let me forget about him?"

Many times she would smile, and say "It is so pure from you. It is felt from your heart, the one true love." Then she would always follow with,

"Try and stay focused." Other times she would ask me to ask myself if I was supposed to let him go.

~The love was so powerful, but the pain of longing did not leave.~

My senses with zooming into the body became stronger. I would touch a person and then see into their body. Many that had visited a doctor were verifying I was right on - I would repeat the results that they already knew. Once these experiences started happening day in and day out, I found myself talking less to Sam. She seemed to honor I needed to do this and we talked when we could.

I was going through so much, and working to let it happen. This left no time to be on the phone with anyone.

Back then, tears flowed and I would sink into sadness. Not only was the spinal pain continuing, now it was joined with the beginnings of stomach pains. The pain would be so intense that it would wake me from a deep sleep. I would do my best to restore my strength and would walk into Abigail's office bent over. I wanted something for the pain, but I wasn't one to take any medications - not even aspirin. When this happened, she would give me the only thing I could take, which was a type of homeopathic Aspirin. I did tell her at one point what I was sensing the pain in my stomach indicated. She raised her voice and told me to never say that word again, and I promised her I wouldn't. It was something that frightened both of us at the time. I remember after she raised her voice, she wrapped her arms around me as we cried. I decided after that not to pay attention to the pains in my stomach. I would focus, try to breathe and let it happen. Time would let all of this disappear day by day for me.

Early one evening, I was told to call Rose another woman from the community center. I was to ask her if I could stay the night. I knew what this meant and I was getting, '*it is time to leave*.'

She sensed I was coming exactly like Abigail did. She told me she had already cleared the guest room for me. Although I was still having my own challenges, I was able to work with her on her spiritual growth as I lived with her.

While staying with her, many people came into my life. I found myself working and sensing for many of these people. I started to help others by seeing what was needed for their spiritual growth. I was also taking on a few appointments with others who wanted intuitive readings and some that wanted me to zoom in on their health issues.

I did not feel at this time I was supposed to promote my gifts or myself. Many people were unaware of what I was going through, and what my abilities could offer. It seemed the people that crossed my path were the ones I was to work with.

I did not like to take money for helping others, but many of them gave me love offerings. Still, in my heart, I found the importance was not the money, but the gratitude for all that was given and received. I was not socializing outside of this busy schedule and it felt like I was being prepared and hidden in some way.

I also kept my time busy volunteering two days a week at an assisted living home. I enjoyed calling Bingo and helping with the Alzheimer patients. When I spent time with the Alzheimer patients, I realized they seemed stuck - stuck in a past moment or time period. I loved sitting with them and letting them share their experience with me. It seemed that they had a particular visual in their minds and it was the only thing they were able to voice and focus upon. To hear their stories, reminded me of the time I laid on the bathroom floor repeating over and over the vision with Jesse. That is exactly how I felt; I felt I could not leave that time and I was stuck. I could honestly say I related to what they were feeling; I honored all they were going through.

I also enjoyed the days with the other residents sitting on the rocking chairs out front. I loved the experience of listening to stories of the past. Maybe, it is because I also loved to share my experiences and my stories.

I was able to escape into the days, leaving the long moments to the night - moments of intense pain in my stomach and moments that my heart still cried for Jesse. Especially, when I would think about him, I would fall into a silence of the room and cry. I would see him so clearly and would feel a longing to hold him. He would appear out of nowhere into my mind, and I could feel every ounce of him. In many ways it felt like he was a part of me. I could not explain the longing for him anymore, it seem so surreal. I was so caught up with the illusion of thoughts linked to him it made me cry. However, the thoughts seemed to follow with such beauty and peace that I would not want them to disappear.

In the thoughts it felt as if we were together, but reality was not matching. I tried to stay focused as much as I could while trying to balance the whirlwind of thoughts.

At moments I would try and capture a small part of who I used to be. Only one moment, a glimpse of what I used to feel like. As it seemed, I was in fact slowly turning into that transparent shadow. I was vanishing into my own illusion. That illusion that did feel right only in my eyes and made the normal life disappear. The illusion that everyone was trying to get a glimpse of to be able to touch for a moment. I was residing in it through my thoughts and safe place of my visuals.

I remembered one day I was guided to go to the mountains. The girl I was living with gave me a tent and a cooler. I loaded the jeep with the tent and some food. I was getting that I could not have any contact with anyone - I was to only write, and listen. I did not even know where I was going. This placed me in some frustration, yet I listened. I did not even know how to put a tent together. I followed as I was guided to go, and my guidance led me to a place to camp. It was actually a nice place, very isolated. I figured out the tent, and learned on my own to start a fire.

I stayed for 11 days, hiked and took on the wild of learning how to survive alone in nature. One day, I was guided to walk down a path and down a hill. I moved the bushes that draped my way and went down. Thinking, nothing is here in this remote area, but then I heard water. I made my way through the trees, and weaved my way past some smaller magnolia trees. It was beautiful, the stream, the sun hitting the water, and the view of mountains towering overhead. I took my boots off and let the cool water run over my feet. It was such an experience to feel one with the water. It felt good, as I sat observing the feeling. To feel and see how everything that touched my feet was connected.

I wrote page after page my emotions and thoughts. After the days were up, I was getting, *go to the top of the mountain.* I took the jeep up, and did not know what to expect. I saw a bridge that went from one mountain to the next. I have always been afraid of heights; it was such a fear with me. Then I was getting, '*walk the bridge.*' I voiced out loud, "You have got to be kidding. No way am I going across that swaying bridge." I sat for over an hour writing, and focusing on my breathing.

I wrote about my thoughts and fears of how foolish I must have been to even think I could do this. I had so much anxiety that started running through my body.

Finally, I listened and took the first step, holding on to the side of the bridge for dear life. I walked slowly across with my heart racing the entire time. Once on the other side, I sat down quickly on a large rock. I felt glued to the rock and did not want to move. I sat and was told to focus. I could feel something inside of me pulling up. I could feel anxiety inside of me, it seem to race up out of me. I let it go, and then looked back at the bridge. The fear released; it was as if I never had the fear at all. I stood up and walked back across the bridge. This time not having to hold on, and walking strong each step of the way. I realized I was not scared at all. I took myself back over the bridge a few times, each time with no fear. What an experience, it worked and I was grateful I listened.

Many different fears kept occurring while I lived with different friends. Each time I was guided on how to handle it. Each time it proved itself to release and the fear was gone, leaving that void of emotion. The emotions that used to take me over so many times before were no longer tucked within me.

I moved again, with some other friends - fifty minutes away from Abigail's house. This place was familiar, the old farm house that Sandy and Charlotte owned. Like the others, they knew and sensed I was coming. They welcomed me without hesitation.

When I arrived at their place, I was much stronger. Each time I was guided to move, there was an exchange of help and understanding from both of us. Each time I lived with someone, they seemed to be aligned with the spiritual awareness to understand me. In turn, I would help them identify, and wake up to spiritual awareness that lay dormant within them. I would zoom in on things for them, and get guidance of what needed to be done to help them grow.

While living with the couple in the country, the tearful hours crashing on the floor had lessened. I was gaining more control over my emotions by interacting with the physical presence of beauty around me. I loved being outdoors around their house and spent most of the days in their yard. It was very peaceful being in the trees and way out in the country like that.

This was not an unfamiliar place of memories for me. Being in the yard brought up memories of my first night with Jesse. It was ironic, it had been exactly a year since Jesse and I camped out here for the bonfire. Even though, that night he related he was a past life and that drama lingered around me, I still remembered the loving memories we shared in the yard around the fire.

After leaving the couple, I began to see a pattern with the length of time living with the people who opened up their homes to me. This pattern consisted of living with each one for three months. During the three month spans, I was introduced and exposed to more social events and people.

These events brought me to establish and form a few close friendships. I found that each time I was in their presence, I would channel information and they would write down what I voiced. I was consistently voicing words that made sense and understanding for our paths. We had long hours of channeling, and long hours of talks about my going to India. Each time I spoke to them about India I felt waves of comfort - it felt like home for me. I did voice over and over, India was a link to home. I was still in a space of feeling I was leaving for India soon. This thought of India stayed with my senses, yet I did not know when or why I was going. The ironic thing was that Jesse left for India months prior to my last move. I had heard he left, and no one seemed to know when he was coming back. I felt strongly I was going to see him over there. I had visions of us there, and this seemed to make me want to go even more. Was it true? Would I see him when I got to India? I had no idea, but I was not going to push leaving too soon. I was not going to get on the next flight, because of what I was sensing. As much as I wanted and had hope that I was right, I was not going to push it, if it was not aligned for me to go yet. I would know when the time was right to go. I knew that I would get the guidance strong when it was time to leave.

I started spending more time around the ones that helped me grow. Many people crossed my path, and I would learn from them. I would listen to guidance and follow, being guided to go to certain places, and even certain people to talk to.

The end of the year was coming, and I remember opening my email one day. There was an email from him. This was the first contact from him I had received in almost a year. I was so nervous. Did I want to read it, was I even ready to hear what he had to say? He relayed an incident that occurred when we where together, about a type of internal healing he went through. He mentioned India, and said he hoped that I would join him. I could feel my entire body heat up, and was scrambled about what to say to him. I responded back, telling him I had been learning and growing quickly. I told him I would love to connect in India, if that is what was meant to be. I sent the email, and thought, 'Why now, why after all this time?' There I went again analyzing it all, 'Stop, Now' I told myself.

I continued on living with my friends. I spent my days trying to keep busy, raking leaves, doing their yard work and learning to be silent. Being outside for me was soothing; nature seemed to help me stay grounded. I kept referring to the word "grounding." I learned much about the word after voicing to Jesse about how he kept me grounded. After our time together, I learned certain ways to help me stay grounded. I had a certain type of visual I would do during meditation, which helped me link to the earth for grounding. It kept me balanced in reality and from becoming so out of it with all the channeling. When I was not grounded I felt a dissolution and separation from reality. I would be guided to eat certain things that help with this. Certain foods had a way of balancing all the energy flowing through my body. The energy would get so intense that I would shake or feel hot surges coursing through me. I would get guidance to learn to be still, loosen my body and just sit. I seemed to be in my own way of letting it all happen. If I was guided to run I would run. If I was guided to meditate I meditated. One time I was even guided and taught the proper steps to take to stand on my head. I realized all of these techniques were gifts and tools for me so that I could balance the flow of the energy better in my body.

Even when I was guided to meet one of my friends, I did, which would lead into a whole realm of channeling new information of awareness. It all seemed to form a way to trust the inner self. The guiding and listening seemed more like a healing than a hinder. Each time I was guided to do something and listened it would prove itself beyond anything. It was like being within my own system, listening and trusting in what I could.

Then one day it finally came strong, '*Time to get your shots.*' It was repeating over and over, I called a friend that I had been spending a lot of time with. She went with me and held my hand through the unbelievable amount of shots that were needed for India. We got it done! After coming back from getting my shots I started channeling the "Elders".

They told me everything I needed for the trip, voicing to me at one point I needed a pack. I remember my friend laughing when I asked her "What did they mean by a pack." A backpack, she told me, to be able to hike around India. I thought you have got to be kidding. I told her I already had my suitcase with wheels ready to go. I did not know this trip involved hiking all through an unknown territory, how is that possible.

By this time she was laughing hysterically, telling me you can't roll your suitcase through the dirt streets of India. I asked her how was I supposed to get everything I needed in one backpack to go to another country. For all I knew I was staying in the country for awhile. I didn't even know how long this journey of my guidance would be - could be a week, could be a month, could be two... I was not sure.

All of a sudden a sharp pain startled me and brought me back from all the memories. I looked down and saw the pen in my hand, with nothing written. I guess I was lost and absorbed in all my memories of thoughts. Now the background noise began to come into my awareness. I heard sirens and the busyness of the city. The city had faded while I was captured in my mind with thoughts. I was sitting back in the room looking around, back in the place I am at this very moment, thinking, 'memories how they stay with us so much.' I cherished the memories of those moments with him and moments with all I endeavored. But, I knew in my heart from the guidance and awareness, I needed to do this on my own.

After my pain released from my stomach, I wrote down some of the things my thoughts brought to my attention. It was helping to get it out, and let it be. I grabbed the pen to let my hand write freely and closed my eyes to let myself remember the rest of the memories.

Right after I was guided to get my shots I was getting, '*It is time to go at the end of January.*' This left only twenty two days to get all that was needed done before it was time to go.

I was guided not to live in one place for more than two days. I was getting that I could only stay with a friend for two days, then move to the next. I would keep my clothes in my jeep and live from what I needed.

To some, this would seem ridiculous, but the ones I was around, honored it. They knew I followed and they understood and could see the importance. I started to see a strong pattern of things. It was so obvious to me that I could not miss it. More and more things followed in a pattern line. The preparation of leaving for India was a year long endeavor. The month before I left for India I was in more contact with Jesse, emailing back and forth.

When the guidance came in, 'almost time to go' my friend decorated a shoe box with, Give Hope to India written all over the sides. I began to put the love offerings from appointments into the box. I kept trusting and following a complete unknown guidance to follow. I knew whatever amount was in that box, that is what I had to take with me. I trusted the amount in the box would provide enough to travel in India. I left for India the second month of the year. My ticket to India was given to me by a close friend.

I traveled and hiked in India for over five months and Nepal for a little over another month. I viewed and studied carefully all the different religions and respected the way of culture. I visited and helped children that were on the streets. I went to the orphanages, and tried to experience all I could with the way of their living. I was even blessed to be able to guide and teach a class of Tibetan children a meditation.

So much could be expressed with the details of the journey and how many people crossed my path. I learned more and more about my ability. The lengths of lessons I learned and the healings that I did, strengthened me. I was faced with hunger to the point of crying. I valued and learned that material objects were not as important as the value of life.

People that needed healing would cross my path and I would listen and complete what was needed. I did have challenges of trusting, I believed this was because I was in a foreign country. This was my first time out of the country, and it was in fact hard. I will always admit the hardship of that, but I am so grateful I listened. I could go on and on with the million adventures.

This would include the experiences along with guidance and along with the ones that crossed my path to give me a message. Guidance would say to me, '*Trust the means of survival, you will be provided for.*' Then I would meet someone, do work with them, and out of kindness they would provide meals for me. People wanted to give back, and the journey continued.

~This led me on a powerful journey. ~

This also led me to meet Jesse and travel with him for one of the months. In the first few months I was in India, he was in Thailand. Then I received an email from him saying he was coming back to India. I was so excited, he said we should meet up and told me where he was going to be. I was in the southern part of India and I had been working on a project of writing a book. I actually channeled the information for a book and had completed it.

When looking at a map, he was going to be right across from me. I thought this would be it; we would be in India together. But then, I was guided to go north. I felt my heart sink; now I would be north, and he would be south. That is, of course, if I listened; but being with him seemed more of what I wanted. I was torn between listening to my heart, and listening to my guidance. The pull with my guidance seemed stronger than ever the last few months. The following and listening led me to meet some amazing people.

~I wondered, 'What to do?'~

Even with the placement of emotions, I knew I had to listen. I was already in such a strong place of trusting the guidance, so I headed north. I trusted so much; yet, I did feel tired and doubted in some ways what I was doing all of this for. It seemed my faith was constantly challenged.

I figured if I was supposed to see Jesse, the Universe would bring us together. I would know; I felt that strongly with all my heart.

The contact with all my connections back home helped with all the disillusion of what I was facing. I used the internet as a bridge between continents to receive the support of friends back home. It was scary at times, and I did find myself losing so much weight and losing the faith that followed with keeping up my strength. How could I feel the faith being lost, and still trust so strongly? I got a bus ticket to go north, but really wanted to just go home. Go home, or go to meet Jesse, opposed to traveling alone.

I was learning so much, and watching the lessons right before my eyes. I guess the thoughts of him kept me going and moving forward. I could still feel so much love, and I was still in the illusion of what I would see in my mind. I felt like at times I was making up such a fairytale that did not seem real. 'Was I seeing future visions with him?' I would often question myself. Every time I would have a vision I would try and pop him out and remove him from what I was seeing. He would then reappear, so I started letting the visions come. I would observe them, and let them come, Jesse in all.

As I traveled North, I had so many experiences of seeing things with people. Something new started to happen to me, it was different. I have been able to see into the body and identify the illness or injury. Now, I was seeing why the injury or illness had occurred. I was also seeing what future impact the injury could have on the body. Many times I would do hands on healing with energy. Now, as I was healing I would see, I would see how it could be related to future issues. This was new for me, and then I would start to see exercises that would help that person prevent or heal the injury.

In one particular experience, I met this guy and was spending some time with him. I was seeing issues with his right foot; I told him and he said I was correct. He told me his right foot collapsed, and that he had been to many doctors, but they said nothing could be done. I saw future issues with the spine, because of this injury. I asked him if I could sense for him and he was willing to give it a try. So I would get a healing visual in my mind, then we would follow the guidance. I saw him sitting in a chair, so he did. All of sudden I would ask him to sit a certain way. Then I would see moves in my mind and he would try them. This process unfolded and the images would appear. I was seeing a bright light running from his lower spine to his foot. Then, I would see how he should hold and angle his foot. I saw an image of him taking his thumb and pushing in on the area in an upward position. I voiced to him, to imagine in his mind that the foot was healing. This went on for over an hour, and I worked with him in different positions that were good for gaining the strength back in his foot. It was an amazing experience, and he was very grateful. More and more this was happening with different people. I was traveling like this for awhile.

Then one day Jesse asked me to meet him in central India in a town called Varanasi. After that he was going to a place that I had wanted to visit, but I didn't know if it was time for us to meet, yet.

Finally a few days after the email I was getting a loud, '*Yes.*' and '*book the train ticket.*' I was getting he needed to meet me at the train station. I felt maybe the reasoning for meeting at the train station was because the town was not very safe for a woman traveling alone. I did not want to have any expectation with meeting him. I already knew how I felt, and I was so excited. It seemed so right, and I felt much stronger by this time.

After all the excitement of knowing we were meeting soon. I thought about the first time I met him - I thought about all the things that came to me while I was away from him that whole year up until now. Reminders and thoughts kept popping into my mind.

It seemed and I felt that I needed to get to a certain awareness level before we could connect together. I knew that I had been going through some major stuff with cleansing. I did not know, but felt maybe in some ways it would harm him to be around all the emotions that were coming out of me. He was sensitive and aware so I felt he would be able to feel all these things. I was getting stronger with understanding and I knew I was releasing some major stuff. I know that when this happens that it is not good to be around people. This was not at a good energy level. I was in a lower vibration; this to me meant that my energy was at a low place. One's that are sensitive to energies could feel this. In some ways it does affect them. So maybe, this was some of the reason for all the time that has gone bye. I do believe in my heart that there is more in depth understanding to it all. A reasoning I guess I should not know right now, but I was getting, '*Before your energies can be around each other, a certain level needs to be reached.*'

Who knows reality was still not matching for me, but all of this started to come together in some small way.

I wanted to work stronger on understanding the visions of the future. I was hoping to get some time line of awareness with it. It did seem like I was in the illusion all the time. I was seeing and feeling one thing, and for the last few years I was in my own world. This has seemed to take on my existence, and I was following and trusting.

We talked before it was time for me to come to Varanasi. He said he would find us a guest house to stay in; I told him to find a quiet secluded place if he could. The noise was really getting to me; my senses seemed to be magnified. He was so sweet, and seemed excited that we were going to meet. I guess I did not know that for sure, maybe it was just me that was overly excited. Then again, he had been away from home for over a year, so seeing a familiar face would be good for both of us.

To me, he felt like he was so much of my future; such importance that I could not even understand.

What was all the importance with it, and was I just making it all up? I knew I should not dwell on the future. It was more about being in the experience of that moment and that time. I wanted to enjoy each moment with him.

I headed for the train; it was going to be an eighteen hour ride. I booked to stay on the sleeper part of the train. This consisted of bunk beds that pulled down from sectionals inside the train. I kept myself busy writing, and reading all that I had written so far.

I arrived as the evening hours began, with thousands of people wandering around the station. Thinking how is it even possible for him to find me. India was different than what I was used to. I was used to everything being written and spelled out for me, such as getting around with more specific directions in front of me. This was not the case, and with all the people it was hard to find myself in the crowd let alone someone else.

I flowed with the crowed walking down some stairs and saw him looking all around. I wanted to leap off the step, hug him and not let go. It was such a sight to see him, especially after all that I had experienced. The anxiety was bursting through me. He took my pack, and voiced "This is it?" I told him, "I did have a smaller pack also, but unfortunately it was stolen on the train." I let go of all the emotions with the items stolen. It was not an easy thing to do letting the emotions go, I had so many things in that bag that were sacred to me. Especially the only copy of a notebook filled with two years of poems.

We headed out of the station, and negotiated a rickshaw ride back to the guest house. I changed and we......

All of a sudden there is a piercing in my ears and I hear a ringing sound. This brings me out of my thoughts and writings. Then, as I focus and get clearer I realize where I am, back in the city. Not in India, but back in my present place in America.

I am often able to get into this transit state of thoughts. It is like a strong meditation state while being able to write at the same time.

I looked over at my phone, and realized I was still sitting in the same position as earlier. The same stack of papers on the floor lay right next to me. With a new stack covering my lap.

I had only been in the city for about three months now. It was such a different transition from where I lived, to India, to now in the big city. All three places had a whole different feel to them. Each one had a different energy level, and way of living. This last transition had proved itself in reality more for me. Things in the last few months had been great; I had regular appointments, and even a few workshops. Thoughts of all the people that I have worked with, and all the ones I have helped, made up for all the anguish that was placed upon me over those years.

The joy of helping others was proven for the question asked, "Are you sure this is what you want?" I sat quietly taking in all the gratitude and love I felt for what I have been able to give.

Then the pain in the stomach started again, I bent over and pushed as hard as I could on my abdominal area. I refused to let my senses go there, knowing all that I already knew with what the pain was.

This was a different issue, then helping people and travels with Jesse. I did not want my thoughts to go there, ignoring it right now, I felt was best. I would know what to do when the time was to heal it.

Guidance always comes in when the time is right. I ran a bath, and then headed to bed. I decided to not think or write about the rest of traveling with Jesse tonight. I will finish tomorrow and let the illusion of what was needed go. It did seem it was the right time to let it all go.

Deep within the heart lays a love so true
The distance of a man that she loves forever will be the two
The gratitude for holding him, the gratitude for which stands
beneath the hands of time
She will honor all that is given, with the one of eyes so blue
She places such hope that one will see beneath visions of love in the
distance
See her, for who she really is,
Letting the love of unconditional stand strong in the mere lights
of a sky hidden in an illusion of love that was forever to be true

Chapter VII

LOVE'S ILLUSION

*T*he pain woke me up again and again in the night. I found myself sitting up, and holding my arms around my knees. Finally in the morning, I listened carefully as the guidance came in. I was to mind shift the pain, and circle my inner stomach area with light.

After, I went to finish my memories of traveling with Jesse. I sat quietly in my living room letting my thoughts begin where I had left off. I closed my eyes to get into the transit state and let my mind bring me back to my travels in India. I was back in India to when we were together. I began to fill the pages with more words of my past.

As we got ready for our first adventure out, I kept looking at him. I did not understand. I was standing in front of him and I could not see him. I was trying, but I felt like I couldn't. I had all those visuals and thoughts of him that seemed so real, now he was physically in front of me and I literally could not see him. I felt like I could put my hand on him and my hand would go right through him. It was so weird and I could not explain this different experience even to myself. It seemed so surreal he was finally next to me after a time period of over a year, but he was like an illusion. Was this because I was so used to seeing his spirit that the real thing did not make sense? It was like my fantasy turned into my reality.

After about three days, was when I started to really be able to see him. It started to feel real. One day while talking, different emotions started to pull up for me. He was helping me identify the issues I was bringing up. These were strong emotions that I had not dealt with in the past.

When this happened, the experience and emotion would take me over until I worked through it. It was kind of like when I was in the mountains, and had to walk across the bridge to release my fear of heights. It literally, would had an impact over me and seem to slam me. I called this "crashing." It would take over, and I would get all the emotions attached with the situation.

I did come a long way since I lived with Abigail in the beginning. When the crashing happened, then I would lay on the floor for days. Now, I knew to ride it out, I called it, "riding the wave." So the intensity of this got better, but it still controlled me.

As Jesse and I were talking, he realized he needed to go pick something up. He felt bad to leave me in that state, but told me he would be right back. He voiced, "Maybe, I should get quiet and try to work the thoughts through." After he left, I sat with the thoughts this was always where I could scream and cry all at the same time.

It was unbearably hot outside and in the guest house. I was so thirsty. As I thought about going to get something to drink, I had a visual in my mind. I saw Jesse walking in the street carrying a clear plastic bag of what looked like orange juice. I thought, 'I hope that is mango juice, I really want some mango juice.' I wondered if I was right and thought about going out to get some. I decided, either way I would stay and wait for him. After about twenty minutes, I could not wait any longer for him to come back. Normally I would wait, but twenty minutes of heat felt like hours. I adventured out to get something cold to drink. While I was walking he was coming towards me. He was smiling, and raised his arm up with a plastic bag in his hand. "I got you some mango juice." I was shocked, that visual was so clear and exactly like I saw it.

This kept happening quite a few times with me. Even, before he would speak something, or ask me something, I knew beforehand. I wasn't sure, did I sense it, or did I have a strong connection to his thoughts. It was very interesting.

The same thing happened with him as it did with me. It seemed that every time I would think of something, he would bring it up. On one account, I was thinking about flying home with him. Then he asked me to come back home with him. He voiced that I should consider taking the same plane. I told him that I would see, and I would know if it was time for me to go back. We seemed to be on the same page of thoughts, at the same time.

Eventually, the songs in my mind started playing a role in all this. All through our time together, I would hum songs. Different songs would come to my mind while with him, and I would start singing or humming the words. He would always look at me, smile and voice that it was the song he was just thinking of. Sometimes, I would laugh quietly as the songs filled in my mind. The songs would come out and be a funny way of how I felt at that moment. The one that came in first was, 'I don't want miss a thing,' then followed 'Every day is a winding road' and then, 'You say I only hear what I want to.' I remembered all through our Journey, the one song that stuck with me the most was, 'I can be your hero, baby.' It seemed that I wished he would be my hero in some ways, so this would make me smile. I would laugh, while the mind thing continued with us.

Many things stuck with me, especially some things he would say. I was telling him how hard it was for me being totally out there all of the time. I voiced to him it was hard for me to function in reality and be here. I seemed to be in such a different understanding with reality and more spaced out half the time. It scared me to be that zoned out all the time. He voiced to me that it was easy for him to be in the reality of it all. He looked over at me with eyes of comfort and said, "Then I will have to build you a bridge. I will build you a bridge from there to here."

His words on many accounts made me laugh, made me cry, and made me look deep within myself.

I was not clear about going back to America with him yet. I knew it was going to come in loud and clear when the time was right. It always did, I usually sensed first, and then I would know. I have found after sensing, then knowing, then loud and clear from my guidance. When I know and I have heard it loud and clear, I do listen and follow, and that is it, I go.

He arranged a ten day silent meditation. As we were on our way, I told him I would see if guidance came in clearer whether I could stay or go. I voiced to him that I was sure my senses would be strong while we were meditating. Of course, my choice would be to go back home with him. But, I knew I was following and I knew the guidance of words would be louder, if I resisted. It would repeat over and over, for a strong reason, until I followed.

The meditation was amazing; we had to be completely silent the entire ten days. The layout of the center was incredible; the beauty was so creative in all the buildings. The women stayed in their own rooms on one side of the facility, and the men on the other side. We meditated for about 8 hours a day.

My first night without him, I thought a lot. I remember missing him, because I had spent every day with him for over a month now. It did not feel right being alone that first night. The next few nights were the same; I really missed him. Then one night, as I lay staring at the wall, I started to have a visual. He was with me, and it was such an intimate visual. After the visual disappeared, I started to cry really hard. I voiced out loud, "When I stop this pattern of crying, I do not want to cry ever again."

I had been crying straight for too many years now. After this visual I realized, I was crying because it felt so real and I could literally touch it. Then, I said to myself, 'I don't know if I am crying because it was so real, or was I crying because I was not sure if it would ever happen?' The realness of it felt so right, every touch, every look, all of it. The love that I felt while I was embraced in seeing it was like the waves I felt. Only this wave was peaceful, and it felt like my body was pouring out so much love.

Many things came in while I was meditating. The one thing that came in strong was I needed to go to Nepal. It was strong, and it came in over and over for two days.

"Well, I guess I was not going back with him. He was leaving four days after we finished the retreat.'

Then, after a few days of sensing and hearing to go to Nepal this came in:

~ *Go to Nepal to face your death.* ~

That was all I kept getting again. It was again following the riddle of understanding, trying to make sense of a puzzle. If I listened, what was going to happen? Why would I possibly listen and go face my death?

I remembered thinking when he did ask me to go home with him. 'Was he only trying to get me home to all the other comforts.' I did not care anymore about the comforts, the material of it all. But, I did care about him. I would say to myself, "Let's see, go to Nepal to face my death, or go home with the man I was in love with." Not a hard choice. Yet, it did have factors at both ends of it. I had not stopped listening, and I was being guided strongly. Facing my death, meant what? Was I going to die, and who would chance that? Going home with a man that maybe, I could have hope, that he may care for me in some way.

After the meditation, I waited and we met at the front gate. He walked up smiling, and said I looked very peaceful and my energy looked amazing! Then came the question, I had spent the last few days trying to get a clear answer with,

"Can you come home with me?"

"No, I think I have to go to Nepal," I replied even though I did not want to answer. It was so hard to hear it being voiced aloud.

I knew in my heart I would listen, it is who I am. I think that I did know fully in my heart, at that time, this was something that I could not turn away from now. I could not take any chances of not following and seeing if this was real or not.

I believed on a higher and stronger level he helped me. I guess all this awareness really came to me when it was time to leave him.

We had less than a week left together. He asked me if I was excited to go to Nepal. I could not feeling the excitement of it. The last few

days with him were just what they were. I was too disoriented to realize anything those last days. At one point, I reached a place within
that was so deep. It pulled out some things that I had experienced
physically, that I felt I was over. Yet, when it pulled out, I realized the
pain was still there. These few experiences fell into the lines of being
taken advantage of. I don't even want to write it, for it was something
that happened in my reality, and something that does not need to be
put into words anymore. These were very painful experiences for me,
and very tragic ones in my eyes. What started it all pulling up, was
something that he said to me, which lead to one of the events.

This event occurred a few years prior to that moment. It was a
physical thing that happened to me, and for some reason his words
made it come to the surface. I remember crying, as he held me tightly
when I told him what happened. While I was telling him, I could feel
all of the pain from when it occurred. It was so intense for me and he
quietly listened word for word.

After I voiced it, we laid there, with my head buried into his chest
which was wet from all the tears. His arms were still wrapped tightly
around me. We let the silence flow through the room, as my hands
grabbed his body. Grasping and praying the pain would surrender.

Then, I let my mind take me back to that physical event that happened a few years ago. I could not feel it anymore. The emotions of
pain with it were gone. It was like a complete void inside of me.

The next morning, I went down and ordered us breakfast. I wanted
to get it back to the room before he woke up. I ordered pretty much
everything on the menu. I carried some of it up, set it on the bed without waking him and then went to grab the rest. I woke him, and we
had our last breakfast together. He had such an appreciation for food,
it made eating more joyful to watch him.

It was time for me to go; I bought a small backpack to carry a few
changes of clothes. I got my large pack ready, since Jesse was taking it
back for me so I didn't have to carry it to Nepal. He walked me to the
train, gave me a hug and said,

"I love you," and walked away.

I remember sitting on the train and panicking. He was flying home
that same day, and I wanted to run off the train, to the airport. My
heart ached so badly, and I guess, I started to feel some anger. I did

not want to go face my death, whatever that meant. I wanted to take a chance, and hope he would see me for who, "*I am*" and just love me.

On the train I began to write:

As I summarize the month an a half I spent with Jesse, I guess this brings most of our time into the light of it being the complete whole.

It did hurt at times with him, he did voice to me he did not want to be with me. I was crushed when he voiced this to me. I did not know how to respond to any of it. Was I that off? How could I be that off when everything else seemed right on? How could the one thing that seemed closest to my heart, be wrong?

This made me frustrated so many times; maybe I made it all up. Maybe, none of this happened; I was so sure with him. I had visions, some very intimate, and the love in these visions was so powerful. With Jesse, my heart and visions showed an illusion of something different. I had made up an illusion for so long. I believed he had to step away from me when he did. I believed, he was not supposed to help me, and I had to do it on my own. I believed so many things. But, it was all the story I created to get me further on my journey. I said I trusted, but did I truly? If I had, then I would not have doubt or reason for analyzing it anymore.

We traveled, and I seemed to be crying more than I wished to be. He was saying things to me and that brought up emotions to deal with. I finally realized that by him doing this, he was reaching things deep inside of me. I could feel it, and it was being pulled out of me, so I could release it fast.

These were things that I know now, were so deep it probably would have taken a century to come out of me. I wanted so many times, when I was with him, to run some place else. Maybe, I wanted to run from the truth of what was right now. I did enjoy traveling. And yes, he made me cry. But, we also laughed a lot, talked a lot, and released a lot. For me, it was so easy to be around him. As soon as we started traveling, it felt like we had never been apart; everything flowed. In some ways for me, it was like we started from where we left off, and all that time in between did not even exist. We flowed together, traveling and getting around in the norm of living. I have to say, it did come easy. I guess, I only voice easy, because for me it has been difficult to function so much in reality these last few years.

For some reason, being with him, I seemed to be able to touch reality a little bit more.

We went with the flow of everything, hours on the train, long jeep rides up the mountain, and even the most unfit sleeping places you could imagine.

We did not travel like tourists; we traveled staying with the closeness of what the culture was about. We connected to the energies and honored the masters that have left us.

I fell ill many times and he was kind hearted about it. The challenges of spending that kind of time together, in the environment that we did, showed me something. It showed me, that in all reality aspects of hard times, we could do it and make it work, 24/7. Even though, we seemed to be working through so many things, those things to me were on a spiritual level. I felt we needed to pull those things out.

I can't quite explain it; I really have never viewed the reality of it all - the norm of how people could have judged it. To me there was no judging, I went with the lessons day after day.

We did have fun; we made the best of it in the norm, and in the aspect of releasing deep things with the spiritual. Being in his presence I felt different, it felt right. It was an adventure in itself, through all that was given.

~To come to a time now surrendering and saying good-bye~

I guess, many times, I would look at him and think he knew what was happening to me. I would lay there with him at night, and stare at the ceiling.

'Wondering, does he know, does he have a clue what I am going through? How can he say he did not want to be with me?'

How could he come right out and say, "I don't want to be with you."

I expressed to him one day that I did not understand. If I was seeing the future, then how is it possible you don't want to be with me? He voiced, "I never said, I did not want to be with you in the future, I just don't want to be with you right now." But, I had to be with the words of what he was saying now. Even though, he was saying it, my heart knew he was right. We could not be together right now. Even if it meant, yes, maybe, later I had to let it go. I had to believe that if it was meant to be in the future, then it would happen. I was to surrender, to all the aspects of it ever happening and coming to acceptance of that.

Besides, how can you love someone if you never get the chance to miss them? I believe if you love something or someone so much, and let it go, it frees it up - freeing it from any attachments of emotions. Letting them go, to be able to learn the lessons that they need to learn and grow within for themselves. Letting it therefore, be shown in your heart that if you love someone or something so much, you are willing to give them up - to then prove, you have nothing more, than an unconditional love for that person.

> *She sits with wonder and holds her heart strong*
> *For knowing he will be the only one*
> *that her heart will always long*
> *She no longer cries for him to see what is to be*
> *Because she knows deep within they both believe*
> *She carries a brightness for all the world to see*
> *For it is him that made her all that she is to be*

I sat quietly on the train as I took in all that I wrote. Well, I guess the poems are not all lost. I seem to be getting some more as I write more.

I awoke in the middle of the night to a few guys talking loud next to me. I was getting something:

'*All that was released needed to be done. This was the last of the cleansing, the last of what was needed to come out. All that happened, was to get you ready for what is about to happen. It was preparing you, and getting you ready for what you are about to face. You need to be free of all those things deep inside. All those things needed to come to the surface for what you are about to experience. He helped you pull up things that no one else could get to, not even yourself. Emotions so far inside of you, but they needed to be released.*'

Still, having no idea what I was about to face, I decided I would trust. I would believe whatever was about to happen was supposed to happen. I struggled with what I felt was the pull of guidance, and how I knew I had to do this. All the things that Jesse helped me pull out, had to be pulled out.

~Guidance was right, I faced my death! ~

As soon as I got to Nepal, I was bitten by an insect. I developed a high fever, became lethargic, and began sweating a lot.

I had a high fever for seven days, and did not have the strength to leave my room. I started to ask what it was, and it came in loud and clear:

'A poisonous spider bite.'

I found the bite on my leg, and trusted I could heal the fever. During the time of the fever, I was seeing some horrible negative things. "Was I really going to die here?"

For days I would write and I was grateful that when I was with Jesse, I was guided to buy a novel on the streets in New Delhi. I began reading it and it helped to draw the negative thoughts away. I would try and bring positive thoughts into mind - thoughts of my mentor's words, thoughts of the people I have helped along the way.

I would lie back, and remember the first time Jesse kissed me. It was one of the last few days we spent in India, and I was telling him about facing my death. I was telling him a story of what I wanted if I was to die. We were laying on the bed, and I was voicing it to him. Then he leaned over gently towards me, and kissed me. The kiss naturally fell into the moment. It was the gentlest kiss I had ever had. It came right at the perfect moment of compassion. It was like the very first time you receive your first kiss. This kiss helped me close my eyes at night while dealing with the fever. It would help me sleep to see him kissing me good-night.

When the fever let up some, I was guided to take a bus to another part of Nepal, called Pakora. I booked the bus ticket, and emailed everyone to let them know I was fine. The bus ride was a long five hours, especially since I was still feeling ill. When I got there, I wrote, and I felt how it would feel if I was to die. I literally felt it, and was getting, 'You are experiencing all the stages of death.' I thought at least if I was going to die, I would die with beauty surrounding me. The village where I was staying was very quiet. A small place, it was surrounded by enormous mountains, and a beautiful lake. The lake seemed to wash over the land with its grace, beauty and peacefulness.

So I wrote all of the experiences, of what I was feeling. But each day my leg got worse. Finally, after it started to get really swollen and my leg turned black, I could not walk on it anymore. I showed the man that owned the guesthouse my leg and he took me to a doctor. It was an open stall clinic that was set right on the road. Literally, wide open, and a doctor came out from behind a curtain.

They treated me so nice, and I was grateful I was there. He voiced to me what it was. It was in fact a poisonous spider bite, and they wanted to cut it open. He said that the poison must come out of my leg. I guess this was the part you can say, I finally freaked out about the bite and was stubborn. I had seen way too many movies about unsanitary knives. So, I would not let them cut my leg open and went back to the guest house.

Meanwhile, I met a guy that was traveling, and we had become friends. He had been hiking all through the mountains, so he was well equipped with survival tools. He handed me some things that I could use to cut it open, including some bandages.

He offered to do it for me, and I told him "No, I will do it." I went to the front desk of the guesthouse to give them a letter I had written. It was an emergency contact letter in case anything happened to me. I asked them to please check on me, if I did not come down in the morning. They voiced it would be no problem, since the guest house was pretty empty.

I burned the knife he gave me, bought some rubbing alcohol, and cotton. I went back to my room, and sat quietly to clear my head. I rubbed the area really good with the alcohol, and then twisted up one of my shirts to bite down on. For several days, the area had festered and formed a mound the size of half an orange on the side of my leg.

I made a small cut in my thigh, and the poison started to pour out. I listened to guidance the entire way through while I laid on the bed.

I squeezed what I could out, with my leg tipped so it could seep onto the bed. Giving it a few minutes in between, then squeezing some more. I then poured the alcohol into the wound. I bit down as hard as I could as the tears streamed down my face. The hole in my leg opened up to the size of a half dollar. I felt like I was going to faint. I got up and hopped to the bathroom, and splashed water on my face. I then covered the hole with some gauze. Then I wrapped my leg with some ace bandage.

I made myself stay awake, and then my friend came down to check on me. I had asked him earlier to check on me in case I did not come out of my room. My room was infested with small ants, so he helped me devise a plan to keep them away from my leg. I was afraid they may burrow into the wound. He stayed for a few hours and made sure I was Okay.

Afterwards, I focused, and did some energy work on it, and then fell asleep.

In the morning, I was able to get up, walk downstairs and say good morning to the owners.

They were happy that I was alright, and offered me some tea. I did not venture out much for a few days; I stayed in and wrote. I was going through so many thoughts with death. It seemed that I was getting so much energy, that it's intensity would come out of nowhere and hit me. Sadness, anger, frustration, loss, it was all rising, and I was expressing it all on paper. After a few days, I felt I was losing my faith. I did not want to die alone. I was scared as my mind raced with so much of these emotions.

I started to let all of my internal emotions come out. I searched for every outlet of strength I could. Writing seemed to help in the most miserable times. I let the poems again start to unfold, and wrote a few about death.

PROCESS OF DEATH
You fear the unexplainable
You fear what is to come
You sit in the glory and peace
Of all that you have loved and all you have done
Your mind takes you to each moment
that life has given you blessings
A moment you felt the sweet embrace and hugged your child
A moment you have given all your faith to help and heal a person
A moment you have felt that soft kiss from the one you hold so dear
A moment you realize death should not be a fear
Then that moment you have closed your eyes
And accepted the time is near

RIGHT BEFORE YOU DIE

Time is a lifeless form of existence
Your mind, body, and soul has no comprehension of anything
You cannot feel touch or sense anything
You lay alone, remembering a soul once told you, you are never alone
You feel as if you have already reached the other side
As you are the lifeless form, floating on a cloud
You have no worries, no fears, no doubts, NOW
No attachments, judgments, or fulfillments
Breathe, close your eyes
Smile and know, life was exactly the story you created it to be
No blame, no pity, just be
Then the light will be the expansion to set you free

I wrote over and over each night my feelings and what I was experiencing. I started to see a pattern and watched more clearly as it came.

One night I wrote with such despair as I was curled up in my bed. I was praying to stay alive and losing my faith fast. Not even believing in any of this anymore. The extreme of the words came,

'As I lay here in my room staring aimlessly into the stillness of the air, I want to convey the words in my mind out. I sit in a wonder of disillusion, an illusion of what is real and what is not.

I have been ill for many weeks now walking in despair of "Why am I here? Why should I be tested in such a way?" Nothing makes sense anymore.

The room is stuffy with a deep stiffness in the air. I hear the faint sound of the rain outside, which seems to be endless these last few days. The fan overhead is circling slowly, with such loudness going around and around. As I lay curled up on the small bed next to the window, I sink into the thoughts of death and the thoughts of him.

The words he has spoken seem to ponder in my mind. The action of this illness has taken over my body. Yet, my heart cries to be free from the thoughts my mind is creating from both of those right now. How is this all happening to me?

~My heart does not seem to have awareness of what pain it is bringing to my mind. ~

My heart feels so much love for him, but reality brings the thoughts of pain. I relapse over time with him and it brings me to wonder "Why?" Why have we encountered each other again? Then, I find myself going back to my visions of him. Was it such a story, made up to only help me through all my transformation? Was it an illusion of hope, to bring me to work through all the deep pain inside? Or has this freed me of the hardship caused by my ego? He has brought me too much freedom. Much freedom of the suffering inside. Yet, the suffering I invoke right now to let him go is more revolting then I can describe. I feel a void inside of me that I have never felt before. It is as if the story has died.

The story I had made up to hold hope. The story in which, I wanted to believe to be true. Why, would I hold such an attachment to it? When, I know I have learned from him about attachment, and basing your happiness on someone else. Now, I know it has many meanings. I started this with faith; having the faith to believe in what I am following - having the faith to believe in helping and healing. I did put such a strong emphasis on following with my guidance. I still hold in my heart my compassion for that. Yet, my last few days have been in question of all of this.

I left him weeks ago, knowing and feeling it was time to move on. It is time to accept fully what I want to do here. I sit thinking about when he asked me to come back with him. That played in my mind, 'why' another 'why,' following a question of non-understanding. I sit here smiling at that very statement I wrote. I have had many times when that 'why,' came to follow a question of non-understanding and I seemed to keep going.

-Going into a forward of the unknown. -

Looking back brings me the pain, yet some of the things I look back upon hold so much placement. Placement of where I was going to be.

Knowing at times I have no home, no foundation, where do I even begin to start. Yet, yes, many people have to start over. I guess I have blamed myself, for my own actions I have taken to following a blind faith. A faith to completely trust and have it worked out, aligned and provided for me to help and heal.

Should I surrender at this very moment to all these
we think are real? What is real? Being here in Nepal, I
so much of society. The programs of real or what we do
The one thing that does strike me different is the moth
The mothers are the workers and it is normal for her to l
ily to do her work. I guess this did strike me coming from living in the
western part of the world.

The ways of living are different here, and not frowned upon as they
would be back home. Do we have to believe that a mother does not
love her children and is portrayed as bad. Only because, she is not
caring for them the way society believes she should be? I have found
that a lot here; mothers leaving their family to do what they need to
survive.

When a mother's love is connected so strong at the heart it can
never be broken. It can never be diminished by society; the heart will
always survive.

Here they believe in the heart and unconditional love. Here they
fend for themselves differently then we do. They do not worry about
material objects or material ways of looking. They are completely in
survival mode. But they do flow with peace, and accept what is, is the
way it is suppose to be.

I feel like our society has lost that simplicity in some ways. Judgments
are harsh, and viewing someone for what they believe seems to be a big
target back home. People form a way of wanting to understand when
a person steps out of the norm of what they believe to be normal. That
in turn leads them to attack the person with ego. Attacking just to
understand why they are taking the actions they are. When in turn
that person is moving forward and following what they believe in.

I am sitting here saying, I take full responsibility of my actions,
knowing deep inside is what matters.

I do believe fully in love, and I believe in what I am doing and I see
all the learning and lessons that go with it.

I was attached to him - attached with a selfish love. He seems to be
a strong element of my foundation. The love in my visions seems to
ground me here. It seemed to bring me into my reality, even though,
they were images in my mind. Those images kept me going and moving through my journey. It is making sense to me now; I am spiritual
in thought all the time.

When he looked me into the eyes I would fully feel that moment. I would be in the now of it and then I wanted that in my reality, bringing my spiritual thoughts into the now. He seemed to bring that balance to me, and for me.'

Page after page I had written, 'Wow, so many words, the flow did not seem to stop.' I finally went to sleep after writing all of this.

On day number three after cutting the wound open, I was guided to take a walk, but I did not want to listen. I was angry, and the listening by this time was what I was not in the mood for. I resisted it as soon as it started saying, '*Go for a walk.*'

After about an hour of it repeating, I gave in and went for a walk and was guided where to go. I went through the village and heard, '*Keep going.*' I came to a mountain as I was walking on the windy road. Getting frustrated that there was nothing there, I wanted to turn around. My faith was lost, and I was not in the mood to walk around. I started to turn around, and heard a loud, '*KEEP GOING.*'

I followed until I reached a restaurant overlooking the water. The restaurant was on stilts, had open sides and a roof made of bamboo. I looked up at the open restaurant and a man sat looking down at me. He was wearing all white, and he waved me to come up. Listening to my guidance, I went up. As soon as I sat down in front of him, I began to cry. He looked at me, introduced himself as Siddhartha, and said, "You have lost some of your faith."

"Yes, it is very thin these days." I voiced with my head down.

He voiced to me that he was planning on leaving a few days ago, but was told by his guidance to stay. His message from his guidance was, '*Stay, she will be coming.*'

"I believe that she is you," as he looked over at me with a smile.

I told him my entire story, all of my adventures until that moment in Nepal. I asked him why he was dressed all in white. He told me that he was silent for three years, and earned the wearing of all white. As I sat with him, I kept hearing, '*Teacher.*'

He voiced to me he was seeing one of my biggest challenges I set up for myself. It was "Love."

That was when I started to voice about Jesse. As soon as I did, I could hear some music. The whole time we were talking, no music was playing. Then all of a sudden, someone was playing music. But,

I could barely hear the song. I listened carefully to hear what song it was. I burst out loud, "No way! That is uncalled for." The song was "I can be your hero," the song I was singing the entire time I was with Jesse. Now, it comes up out of nowhere, as soon as I began to talk to Siddhartha about Jesse.

It did put a simple smile on my face as I thought about him. I was getting signs like that all over the place. They were not hard to miss and over and over kept coming.

I spent three days meeting with the man in white, and he helped to bring my faith back. He helped me believe again in what I was doing and voiced how I was going to help many people. He taught me to honor my gift, and know that I was blessed. By having those three days, and seeing how guidance led me on a path to someone again to help me, it kept me going. I was grateful he listened to his guidance to stay, and that I listened to mine to take that walk.

I felt like I faced my death, to really feel it, and to be able to accept it. I believed that I have experienced all the stages of death, except for the physical dying itself. After my adventure to Nepal, I seemed to accept that if death was what should be, then it was meant to be. I was grateful I listened, and had the whole experience of it.

After I cut my leg open I watched it heal, it made my strength even stronger in believing that I could heal myself. This seemed to be the last of the things I healed for myself on my journey. I did get faced with other things that started at the very beginning. These were illnesses I was faced to get rid of and I listened to my guidance to heal them.

Minor things compared to this: ear infections, urinary track infection, then falling and injuring my knee. But, all these things made me stronger as a healer, stronger in so many ways.

Even in the hardest times, I had the encouraging voices of my friends that helped me move forward.

Many of them would make me laugh, especially my friend Eddie, he would always come up with some comment to turn my thoughts around. Like this one about my bite, "Maybe you should get a small tattoo of a smiley face over the scar. Then you will always have that scar and smiley face on your leg to remind you of Nepal - a little souvenir for facing your death."

My adventures East gave me lessons and taught me courage. Now that I was back in the West, all those preparations led me to understand what I was being challenged with right now. It brought me to this very moment, and I see what I am faced with.

I look around at my small place, with nowhere to hide. My hands reached up for my face to cover my eyes and cry once again. My strength, my loss of doubt, loss of fear; now trusting all will be. I was not sure how to handle this, in this very moment. I was faced with, should I tell my friends what I am sensing with something growing inside of me. Should I let them know, as I write this book of all the events that have happened? All those events make me put two and two together.

Did I have to face my death to experience the acceptance of what happens is suppose to be?

Did I heal to show myself, that I can heal anything that will occur in my body?

So many words left out, but looking at all the words stacked in a pile wondering - where do my thoughts of wonder go? To me it was and is a beautiful love story. From then to now, and for what is to come. There are so many factors of trust and learning along the way, which brings it to the point of having it set in the hands of fate.

I had written so much while Jesse and I spent our time together. So many things, and so much to express, how does one put it all down? How do I write it all?

When the main thing I feel is the focus of reasoning, for writing about the higher understanding into the spiritual world of the illusion? I was taken out of the programmed reality, and was seeing it from a different perspective.

After my time in India and Nepal, I was guided to go stay with a dear friend in Arizona. I was having a hard time missing Jesse. That was when I decided I could not see him. The longing for him was even more intense when I got back. My friend and I spent days talking about my adventures. I channeled so much information, so much was given to help with what was to come. I stayed with her for two weeks, then headed back from where I started from. Back to where it all began when I was getting ready to leave for India.

When I got back, Jesse called my friend and told her he wanted to see me. He voiced to her he was leaving for the mountains and staying behind a few days so he could see me. I did tell my friend I could not see him; I told him that, too, a week prior to my return. I could not deal with the pain anymore; it hurt too bad to see him. Do I keep running from this pain, or face the pain head on? So I thought, 'I guess it is what it is.' Was it testing me to see if the pain was still attached? Was it happening like this to prove I have the strength to let all the pain go? I would have to see, and find out.

A bunch of friends arranged to go out to celebrate my return. We arrived at the club late in the evening. He was standing waiting for us, and as soon as I saw him I gave him a hug. It was hard, since it was the first time I had seen him since we parted in India. The comfort of wanting to be around him came back. I wanted to curl up in the booth with him, and talk like we used to. Yet, I was in this place of being guarded again with myself. I tried to shut off all the emotions that I had with him; shut off the love that I held so strong in my heart. We kept our distance between each other most of the night. A girl approached him and sat with him making matters with controlling my emotions difficult. What was I doing, he wanted to see me, and all that I was getting from him was a few stares. Was he as confused as I was?

Finally at the end of the evening, we sat and talked. I was talking with him, and he reached over and wrapped his arms tightly around me. A wave went right through me, it felt so sad. I was the only one drinking, but I could still feel him as I have always been able to. We went back to a friend's place, and talked more. The night led one thing into the other, and it happened. We slept together, it was not the night I had envisioned, but it happened.

I could feel some blocks from both of us. It seems we, were both blocking each other. Yet it happened, and it needed to be what it was.

In the morning I did not feel right, but I think it was all me. He did come up to me, hug me with a smile and say good morning. I felt that I was having too much expectation of how he should be acting towards me. But then again, I was not even sure how one was suppose to act anymore. I could feel the awkwardness in the room. I should have known it was coming. He was leaving for the mountains, and I was faced with how I would react to it. I did not really react the way I thought I would. It was fine, and I guess I was confused. Did I have expectation's that it would lead some place? Yet, I knew in my heart, that I must finish my journey. And in reality he was not wanting to be with me anyways. So reality and spirituality conflicted once more. I accepted this and was growing stronger to understand, his way of a free spirit with in which he resides.

I talked to him when he came back from the mountains. We talked for over two hours on the phone. Our conversations always mirrored events within our respective lives. The flow of talking with him, for me, could lead on for hours. I enjoyed our views of spiritual concepts which seemed parallel to one another. But as I ended the conversations, I would feel my guard go up and I shut down; he did not want to be with me. His reservation about me made me move forward with everything in a stronger manner.

I was scheduling more appointments, but still having a hard time taking money for sharing my gift. I was helping so many, and that is what was important to me. The appointments and love offerings kept rolling in. Then I was guided to do some workshops with several of the chapters from a book I had written in India called "Powered."

I followed as I was led to do all these things. Then it came in loud and clear to take half of what I was making and put it in an envelope.

I was staying with my friend Mary, during the duration of setting my foundation up, and one of my mentors provided me with a car. I was being pretty well provided for. I was busy and it felt good, doing so much of what I loved. I started talking less to my friends because I had the tools to process on my own now. I found my strength within myself, instead of crying out for help. They understood, and knew this was what I needed to do.

A month after being with Jesse, I was guided to write him a good-bye letter. I really resisted it, good-bye from what? But, I listened and wrote the letter, then took it up to his work. I was with a friend and put the letter in his car. To this day, I don't know if he even got it. But as soon as I left it in his front seat, things became clear to me about love. It opened a door of understanding, and I channeled so much information.

It was some powerful stuff, and it made sense to me. I channeled some understanding for the love:

-Love's reactions and distraction of things. -

Can we have such a love for someone that it places a hold on who we are, and where we are going? At some points it is a stop sign for you, other times it is an obstacle. If you cannot free your self from that love, then it is holding onto your power in a stand still. Holding onto and distracting you from your own views and thoughts of what you feel is right. Most of the time we jump into the other person's views and start to forget our own.

I felt at the beginning of meeting Jesse, he was neither a stop sign nor an obstacle. He was a connection that was needed to move forward. The hold with him came from not letting it go and letting it be free. Being free - which was having no attachment to the way things should be from him. He was the beginning of what was needed for me to help transform all the acknowledgment of love inside.

Transmuting energy of love: I felt the energy of that on a higher level. Now, I must transmute it, let him go and feel the love completely for myself. Feel my love, that was mine in the beginning. The love that I felt and had in the higher realms of spirituality. Now, in order to bring it here to my reality, I must connect physically with that love here. It was like a balance of spiritual awareness of love that is hidden deep inside of us. The love of peace and bliss, igniting as I connect to the physical one. The contrast of the other in the physical to connect balances it out. Feel it like I did then and then release it back to him. Therefore, I can transmute it within myself. Now the love can be found within myself, because it was felt, touched and understood. That love was ignited; now it was my own. Bringing my own love out, to feel the authenticity of it. I wrote this and ironic enough, it made so much sense to me as I felt it. I felt it so deep; it was a love that I know was inside of me. That is something I guess only I can find, without really relying on someone else.

As this was happening to me, I saw and felt many things. I have trusted in my guidance for so long. I trusted and understood. It only mattered that I was the one to understand, acknowledge and accept.

I felt it so strong with him, and now I get how I can feel that within myself.

Another month went by, and I was doing what felt right - helping people. Then I was getting, *'time to go again.'* I did not put up such a fight with tears this time. I was getting where I needed to go, it was taking me to the city. Ironically, I met a girl in India that I had worked with on her spiritual growth. We worked for several weeks and she lived in the city. So I called her, and she said if you are getting guided then please come. I did not question it, if it was going to lead me to make the visions happen, then that is what I wanted. I left for the city after being home for three months. Another three month mark; the three's have been such a strong pattern with me on my journey.

I did have the money to go, so I set off. The first month on my new adventure, I helped my friend understand the "Ego." I was getting an enormous amount of information that channeled in and started writing it down once more. Once again, I still found myself in some frustration of where this was leading me.

At the end of the first month, I was getting to email Jesse. I was feeling I should say to him, "I still walk with steps of you in my heart." So I did, and the response of course was not what I wanted to hear. He did voice that I needed to let it go, and this made me realize I did need to let it go. I was not willing to lay each night of every moment suffering and missing him. Each time I found myself getting stronger, I would fall back into the thoughts of him.

I remembered right before I left my home town, it was coming in loud and clear.

- His spirit will leave you once you get to where you need to be. -

I did not really have the awareness of what that statement meant, until I began this love story. I could still see his spirit, and would have these waves of feeling him so strongly. Maybe much of it is symbolic for me to understand. Was his spirit with me to help me get to where it was I needed to be?

Coming as far as I have with all this awareness, I started to see more in depth of the spiritual realm of thinking. I often wondered with that statement, what physical place I needed to be. If my strength and guidance was so strong, then why was I still seeing him in my mind? I would have visuals and images of his spirit and my spirit standing together on a mountain top. When this image came through, I could feel him, he would hug me and we would sit. These visuals would happen each night, until one evening I saw something different. I was on the mountain top, and his spirit was not sitting next to me. I could see myself in the visual looking around, then I could see him. He was standing about ten feet away from me. Each night that visual would come, and not once would he come over to sit next to me.

Close to the end of the year a major spiritual thing happened to me. It was so in depth, that voicing and writing it all, would leave anyone to question such an unexplainable thing.

I was given a choice with guidance, and with this choice came the ultimate of what I believe was an internal decision inside of me. The internal choice of following all that was pure and good and all that lies deep inside my heart. Most of the choice was to listen to the fullest and go as guided by my higher guidance. I surrendered to make the choice of not letting my ego guide the way. Not letting the ego of fears worry and doubt lead me.

To letting the guidance of the higher good take me on the rest of this journey.

Once I felt this choice inside, I could see his spirit leave. I was sitting on the floor, with all the knowing of this choice. Then my mind went back to the visual on the mountain top. I could see him standing there, and then he slowly faded away, vanishing.

I sat with the love that I held so strong, for so long. I believe in some hidden way of knowing, he did help me get to where I needed to be. He brought me to the ultimate choice of choosing. Then, bringing it to show me that I have all the love and answers inside of me. Those answers are linked to the higher form of guiding. Now, I have chosen to completely let it show me the way.

The love, the seeing, all of it, was absolutely beautiful to me. Yes, I was living so long in that spiritual fairytale of an illusion. But, standing in my reality, it has given me so much hope. It has made me and showed me who "I am." He literally did help change me from the person I used to be to the person I needed to be. That love pulled me through, to find such a different strength of light. To honor all that I have learned and all that I will learn to help and heal.

After that, I did not feel the longing anymore, it was gone. I was told to channel and write another book. Another one, how is that possible? But, I was getting to write it and that it was to be the last book to leave my energy, to make way for what is to come. Interestingly enough, it all seemed to fall into place. When the New Year approached, I was set up with a space to work on the book. I was given an opportunity to house sit for someone, which I did for a month. During that time, I started channeling and it would flow. On day I was meditating, and that is when the thoughts came in strong for the illusion of a love story. Each day after meditation, the unfolding of thoughts came strong for the one that held such a strong love with me.

When the month was up, I took a week to go visit back home. My friend, Mary, told me that she ran into Jesse and was visiting with him a week before I arrived. I asked her how he was. She said he looked good; he looked alive. I was happy to hear that, and she told me he wanted to talk to me. I did make the effort to go over to his place with her. I wanted to see for myself, if it let go. Towards the end of the visit I asked Jesse, "I heard you wanted to talk?" He asked me, if we could get together while I was in town. I told him I would call him, and we would see. I went back with my friend and talked about whether I should chance talking with him some more. I knew that he was still not matching the visuals in my mind. It was Jesse though, the one that I always said, "Held the key."

I was wondering if the significance of meeting with him was only to have a brief connection. I decided I would see how clear I was in a couple of days. The days went by and I was sensing to call him. I called and we made plans to meet. I went over the next day, first thing in the morning.

I was able to share with him some things that have always been left out with the two of us. Deeper understandings of my perspective, and the connection of my experiences with him. I never really felt I should voice to him the depths, like I do with my friends.

Yet, our conversations always flowed and went to another place. As we laid together, I looked at him and voiced,

"I can't have any expectation with what is to happen. Guidance will not let me be attached to anything. Today being with you is a gift."

That is what it felt like, simply a gift, and I wanted to enjoy every moment for what it was. We did sleep together again, and this time it was exactly how I envisioned, and more. I felt so much love with all of it. It seemed different this time with him, we seemed more open to each other. So I let each moment be cherished with him.

On the morning of my last day, I started to have some anxiety. I did not want to go back; to what and for what? It was a struggle and for the first time in years, I could actually feel being around people. I could feel every moment; it was incredible to feel this again. I did not want to go, but was getting I had to. All the way to the airport I kept voicing, "Maybe my flight will get cancelled."

My friend, Mary, laughed and said, "Stop, you will create that." Well, I wanted that, I did not want to go. After checking in, and waiting, I heard an announcement. The flight was cancelled, because of weather. I remember thinking, 'You have got to be kidding me, nice!' I called my friend, and she picked me back up. I had two more days to visit, and was hoping I could see Jesse. I voiced to her, "I wish he would call me in the morning and ask me out. I wish we could do something together."

In the morning he called, and asked me to go to a meditation with him that night and out to listen to his friend play guitar. I was excited since this seemed so much better than the way it had been.

I was leaving the morning after, and asked if I could stay with him. He said he could take me to the airport in the morning. The night was amazing, and it was nice to be close to him like that. In the past, I always felt so much distance from him; he would shut me out in some way. This night did not seem like that at all, and I went with it. When we got back to his place he played the guitar. I would still get so mesmerized when he sang. It was so breathtaking, it calmed me down and it was so peaceful. We realized it was after midnight, and I knew it was Valentine's Day; he looked at me, smiled and said, "Happy Valentine's Day." I was with him, so I was so grateful. I felt the love in the physical; it was something that meant a lot to me. I guess I could not have asked for more, all I kept thinking was:

'Even if I touched this for only a second and held him for right now, I can be grateful for that. I was able to have and touch that for these small moments. All of that meant the world to me, after all these years. I was not going to push it, and try and make it more than what it was. It was perfect; everything about the night and morning was perfect. So now, I can let it be, and focus on what I need to do.'

He drove me to the airport the next morning and we hugged and said good-bye. I was going back, on the love day, I called it. What a good day to say good-bye, remembering all the love that held from the night before and leaving it exactly to be what was to be.

When I got back to my place, things started slow; but I was working intensely with a few people. I was helping them on their path, and they were growing fast. Then, I asked, "Where am I to go from here?" Knowing by now the answers always seemed to come when the time was right, and I would know. I started to feel that I needed to be fully focused on what it was I am to do. I was getting that I needed to do this full force, and be totally focused.

Was it some kind of force keeping me away from him? Yet, that force keeps bringing us back together, and the process of letting go continues.

In my heart knowing if we are to be away from one another, then that is what is suppose to be.

Even though he was making some actions of choices in his reality, he did not seem affected by guidance like I was. I do believe it is all supposed to happen that way, to unfold and align for things to work as planned. At times, I do feel Jesse totally understands me, and at times, I feel he does not understand the pull. I voiced this pull too many, explaining that you just know and feel it inside.

This pull was of listening to guidance and following to the extreme that I do. Trusting in it as it led me in the direction of what it is I needed to be doing. It has already proved itself to the extreme, so the pull was, in fact, taking me in a direction for the higher good. It has been a journey of living with different ones that have taken me in. Working with my thoughts to not relate so much to feeling homeless. And coming to the feeling of how blessed I really was.

After little contact and a brief while, I heard from Jesse. He was coming to the city for a visit.

We went ice skating, and I felt like a giddy kid again, laughing and holding his hand. It was my first time putting a pair of skates on. He was so sweet, and helped me the whole way. We ended the evening going out with some friends. He asked me to dance, and I remembered that is the one thing that always made me smile. Being out and smiling was finally happening without the sorrow of drinking.

I spent the next night with him; we stayed with a friend of mine. I really wanted her to meet him, and it was perfect. He sang a few songs he had written. One of the songs, I don't even think he realized hit me as hard as it did. The words to the song seemed to match something I had been saying for awhile now. It spoke of the word "secret"; I have been voicing the same word to friends. The content of the secret was something that I kept to myself. It was way too far into the future to deal with at this time. I did not understand most of the time when I sensed things with this secret, so it left me in a place of confusion. But, the song really hit home and was beautiful.

It seemed that all through the time with Jesse, many things appeared to be blatant signs. Even though it is possible that he did not see them or relate them to me, I was receiving obvious reminders of him.

One of these instances occurred a few years ago, right after I met him. On this day I was going for a run, and all I could think about all morning was Jesse. I kept feeling that Jesse wanted to have a motorcycle. If I had the money I would get him one. Over and over the thoughts of this came to me and made me feel good when I could see it. I called Abigail because it was so persistent, and I needed to voice it to someone. Abigail was coming over so I went to the grocery store to get things to make us for dinner. As I was standing there, Dean, Jesse's friend walked up to me. He told me Jesse was right around the corner. I talked with Jesse for a short time, and then headed to the check out. As I was standing there, Dean was on the phone with someone. I could here him talking, and he voiced that Jesse was thinking about buying a motorcycle.

I remember standing there thinking, no way did he just say that. Same day I was feeling it about the motorcycle, he was thinking it. Same day I was thinking of him all morning I run into him.

Many times this would happen with Jesse, I would sense things happening to him, and then find out it did during that same time line.

I feel sometimes people say things that are meant for others to hear, but are signs for us on our path.

Overhearing Dean's speaking about the motorcycle that one day was an affirmation for me.

This is how I felt the song was. The song became a sign marker for me and reiterated my thought.

People may say things to us, and they don't even realize they are talking to us on a higher level. Giving us a sign and triggering something deep within us.

That evening with Jesse moved so quickly, and I did not want it to end. Laying there that night with him pulled me into feeling like everything was going to be all right. He had a way to do that with me, and it helped after all that has happened. The scariest part of this journey for me was not knowing anything and trying to make sense of it all. But, then it only took wrapping his arms around me to feel safe - to feel that everything would make sense. These times of connection with him made me feel alive, and escape from all the chaos happening around me. It brought me into an unknown space which was only filled with peace and love.

The next day, I had to step back into the reality. He had to go, and I knew in my heart I needed to keep going. Following into the blindness of the unknown, while I watched the extreme of lives it was helping. Part of me still wanted to go back home and hope it could be. Hope that, we could fall into the visuals I had been seeing. I could not judge it and I was not trying to. I was trying not to let the ego get in the way. I did not want to start analyzing again. But of course, the ego likes to always play its part. So my thoughts took off and began spiraling. If we are really meant to be, then it will be. I wanted to stop over thinking everything with him; like, does he really care for me? It has not been directed in that way from him. I really don't know what he wants. I stopped blaming myself for thinking I made it all up, and I was crazy. More than anything, it is the truth I was afraid of knowing. The truth of right now, but knowing deep inside does hide all the truth of what is real, and what is not.

~ The truth really of only following your heart. ~

I felt at times when we saw each other or talked, he could feel that place. It is a place that the normal eye could never see or feel. It is a place that makes time stand still. Everything around just stops and disappears.

Should I stop trying to make the illusion so real in my world? Trusting and giving it all now to the hands of fate, placing it over to the hands of the Universe. I guess being able to touch that for the time I did, should be enough. It was pure to me, and the gratitude should be able to circle around that.

I honored the deepness of unconditional love that was felt even for those small moments of my reality. I knew that I would keep moving forward no matter what. I knew that right now, the pull was taking me someplace necessary. Going home was not an option, and I did feel my choices had been made.

I sacrificed all hope of a normal, programmed reality and chose to follow my journey - I honored that. I sometimes feel like I signed a contract and that contract could not be broken. It was higher than any understanding of anyone, and I believed in it. I was working with the energy of source and channeling around the clock. If it is leading me to help others, wherever that is, then I will go there. I must trust if I follow, it will lead me in the right direction for myself. It will lead me to what is right, and when the time is right, will lead me to experience that love with another - the kind of love that I feel from a higher place, and now feel coming from within me. I could feel it inside of me; it is a compassion for what I do.

It is a love on its own, and on its own for explanation and under-standing. A key to being, and loving yourself for what is and sharing that love with someone you hold so dear to you.

~It is amazing what your heart tells you when you think you are not listening. ~

I did speak with him a few times. Once again the cycle of us kept repeating itself. Each time I learned a new feeling, a new awareness to help others. Letting go does take time, and if it does keep circling around I believe it does for a reason.

Letting go is not easy, and he was in fact a gift to watch unfold and learn from. I honored all these times we did connect again. Knowing that when the time to completely say good-bye would come. It would come when it was guided to come.

On one account when we spoke it led into that stand still space where everything disappears. I could always feel him when we talked because my senses were strong; sensing people comes with what I do.

At one point, I was feeling some anxiety in my body about something. He led me into a meditation, and right away helped me. I would visualize when he talked, and it was incredible. When we hung up the phone, I thought about how powerful that would be together. I remembered a quote I channeled once that fit this situation perfect.

- The power of two that stands strong, instead of one. -

I stopped the thoughts, so I would not let myself go there thinking about him again. But, my heart was hurting, and it hurt like that when he left.

When I met Jesse I said, "He would be my biggest challenge." He was the biggest challenge they could set up for me. The biggest challenge everyone goes through. LOVE, in every aspect that goes with it. I learned it all - desire with attachment, comforts from another, ego lust, basing your happiness on someone else. I could go on and on with that one word. The biggest thing I learned was how to feel that unconditional love, and find it in myself. I feel the love, peace, and compassion within that comes out of me. I have so much love for all that I believe in, I voice it with the intention and honor all the knowledge that comes through. I have found voicing with compassion and intention, are some of the keys to help. I grew so much by having a conversation with one, and feeling an unconditional love, I evolved to a higher place of understanding. I evolved into a positive person that holds much peace for all things. This has made me trust in who I am, and trust all that was spoken from my guides.

How do I get it all down, so many things of a pattern? So many things I see with my eyes wide open. Many stories and many of my adventures seem to be left out in these writings. All the things that seemed to add together could not possibly all be written down about him.

Now, I was having a whole different thing in my life happen. I am where I am right now, and faced with something inside of me. It is a fear that I have always had, and I must release it to carry on. A fear I will let go of and learn from. When I do, this letting go will lead me to help many people.

This fear will be more in depth as you read on, it will make sense as you move forward.

It seemed that over these last years, I have had to experience things to the fullest. I have experienced things so I can say, "Yes, I do know how you feel." I have seen this in great depths with all that I have been through with guidance and the awareness of everything.

I was able help and guide others on this path as I experienced a situation and learned from it.

Even when this all opened up for me, I knew how it felt when someone lost a loved one and could not talk to that person anymore or say good-bye. This was like the case when my father died ten years ago, I arrived two minutes late to the hospital. I was devastated, that I did not say good-bye to him. So when I saw the spirits and helped, I could feel the gratitude of love from that person. I literally knew how they felt. There have been many other cases with different things on my journey to justify what I experienced to say I truly know how you feel and get the full effect of things. I want to keep helping this way as I move along on this journey.

I stopped writing as I wanted to be in the energy of the words that were coming out on my paper. As I fell into the stillness of the room, I turned my head to stare out the window at the night sky.

It was so clear, as it had been many years ago; but I was now a new person and seeing it with new eyes in this new place that I reside. The sky was still the same, the same beauty that glimmered with the moon. It was full tonight and seemed so surreal - just as surreal as all my visuals in my mind of hope for what may come.

I stood up to go stand by the window, and a sharp pain hit my stomach. I bent over, and found myself hitting the floor. My mind raced as the pain took over all parts of my body. I dragged myself to my bed, and curled up in the covers. I could feel the tears coming down, and imagined they were kisses hitting my face the same way I do when the rain hits me softly. I don't feel sad; I have no emotions for being upset anymore. Yet, the tears still stream. How could I be in a void with knowing I was about to face another challenge.

How do I tell my friends what I am sensing? The thought of the words hurt in my mind as they came up. Then, voicing out loud to myself, "Do I tell my friends what I am sensing?" How would I voice to them without them showing any worry? I don't want them to put any energy of worry into it.

The friends that I have at this point on my journey all understand the importance of energy. We all know that it effects us in so many ways. We all have a certain understanding with how important the faith is for what I am following. We have learned from each other, to stay focused and be positive for one another. So now, how could I tell them that I was sensing I have stomach cancer? Those words even hurt to say out loud.

Was this indeed a fear that I must face? Is it something that I must face in order to surrender into this acceptance? Maybe, I am wrong? Do I have to face this to heal myself, to help others?

I would never zoom in on the area when the pain took over, because of the fear of knowing. The pain had been going on for a very long time, and I would hide it from myself and others. Then I would let my mind wander and think maybe, I was unable to even zoom in on myself. But, that again was proven wrong by me; I was able to zoom in and see illnesses many times before and was right on each time.

My thoughts took over with all these things as I laid their alone. I was given too many signs this could be it. I started to think about all the times that this may be the case with the signs that were given. I remember the day clearly, Abigail yelled at me to never repeat those exact words.

The most recent sign came to me after I was guided to call Casey. Casey is a well respected doctor in the city, and one of the first client's I worked with. After working with him for some time we become really good friend's. At first when I was told to call Casey I did resist. I knew this meeting would lead to knowing more about the illness I was to face head on.

Being guided to meet with people when I was told, started to really come in strong and clear. It always had a purpose, and when I did, it opened up so much knowledge by following through. I always knew it meant something that guidance would have me meet with someone.

Look at the outcome with Jesse. In turn it was a positive thing, but I had times on my path of unfolding where I wondered if I had not listened to have a conversation with him would all of this still have happened. So now I was really looking with my eyes wide open to see the effects of acknowledging the signs. Knowing now, the doubt must be released and the listening was the way I lived. But, it did bring my awareness to the situation at hand. If I met with Casey regarding this many doors would be opened, I truly knew and believed that.

I put the call off for a few days until it came in loud and clear. After the meeting, I was given all the information I needed and would have the lab work done in a few months. Getting all the warning signs justified it for me. I knew it all along; it was no surprise. It only led all the things into what I have been calling preparation.

Did I in fact have to heal myself? So much to prove to myself, is this possible? It does leave me in a place of knowing I will heal; I do believe that with every ounce of me. I looked back at all the sensing I have done on myself while I traveled. All the illnesses I was faced with and zoomed right in on. I was right and healed myself each time, even to the extreme of the poisonous spider bite.

I know in my heart, that what I have already done is for the good. I looked back at all the help that I have been given on this journey, and all the help I have been able to give to others. I honor that I do have a gift, a gift that may help so many. I have to give it a try, as I believe the effect of one, could effect many more.

Since this was brought to my attention with the cancer, it made me process my life as a whole.

It also made me relapse things over from when I first was facing the understanding of death in Nepal.

I let my thoughts escape, as I laid there staring at the ceiling. I was thinking about the time when Jesse first kissed me. I will never forget how it led into the kiss.

The conversation started with us, as we both laid on the bed during the end of our travels in India. I was telling him what it was that I wanted if I was to die. This is what I shared with him,

If I Was To Get Ready To Die;
I would want to hug my family. I would want to help and heal as many people as I could. And I want a kiss from you.

That Way When I Lay Down To Die;
I would feel the loving presence of my family hugging me. I would
know in my heart that I helped and healed as many as I could. Then I
could close my eyes and see you kissing me good-night.

That was a beautiful moment, and I felt such compassion while
telling him this. And, even more so with the kiss that followed.
I did say I wanted those things and they have happened, then in the
past. Now, I am in complete peace and trust for what is, is now in the
present. If I had to say what I wanted for later, I would say,

"Travel to help, Heal, Walk with him."

All of these thoughts and all of these things, seem to make it easier
if I closed my eyes and did not wake up. Coming to full acceptance, of
what is going to happen will happen.
Realizing how blessed, I truly was for all the amazing people and
amazing adventures so far.
After thinking of these things, I closed my eyes and I could see him
kissing me good-night. Maybe now, I should see that as he kissed me
good-bye.

-Letting all the illusions go, setting all the illusions to be free.-

One never does know what the future holds; one can only have
some hope and hold the hope without any attachment. I didn't know
if tomorrow would ever come, but I trust. I trusted I did not have to
know if I was not going to wake in the morning. I started to doze off
as the sounds faded out of the room. With those three words lingering
in the shadows; ; Help, Heal, and Him.

My mind started to fill with a bright light and I could faintly see
small faces of smiles. I started falling into the silence, and vanished
into what seemed like a dream state. A peace beyond recognition.

Falling deep into the illusion of a love story, I walk softly to finish
the ending with that illusion of hope in my mind. And, my heart

filled with compassion, for all the ones I may have helped and healed along the way.

~ To see him standing as we escape into the eyes, and vanish into the everlasting eternity. ~

> *Your eyes remind me of the stillness in the sky*
> *Your smile the essence of the wind that goes bye*
> *Your laugh is the capturing moment that fills my*
> *eyes*
> *Your voice takes me to the quietness in my mind*
> *the light that fills within you*
> *Surrounds the meadows in which I reside*

> *Never an ending only the beginning…*

Trigger the illusion of the memory that was hidden
We always have an illusion to hold the faith and make it stronger to then create that lost memory of illusion in our reality...

Illusion was part of the forward, take the forward to open up the illusion...

Closing Thoughts

❁

I have written my illusion of a love story and have let it go. Love being a strong word. As we view the identification of what we think is a true love story.

The purity of such unexplainable love.

The portrayal of actuality of what we think and feel this should look like. When in fact, it is an internal movement of unfolding that lies within. The process of love to share with others, begins with the self. Internally bringing out all negative concepts of worry, fear, and doubt to bring freedom. Balancing purity and finding that place of love tucked deep and hidden in yourself.

I am not real, you are not real, we are two illusions walking around trying to find the freedom within ourselves. Let the spirits walk as two, to come together to be one. A whole of an illusion to form a physical union, to be a divine of true purity. Now I have let it go to be set in the hands of fate.

The rationales which stand in time can never make up for the leaving behind.

She captures a moment of twilight so blue, to find herself escaping to the heart that stands true. Escaping into the illusion which stands in her mind.

Hope Rechea

As One Story Ends, Another Begins

This was a journey, that extended from being a normal person with views of the standard way we all perceive things. To feeling like a child does when things are new, the new feeling of "should I be excited" or "should I be scared."

My experiences at first were very difficult for me to even admit, let alone, voice to others. How could I possibly come to accept telling people all that I have learned, is an inner journey through the realm of the spirit world.

Spirits teaching me and guiding me to trust in something that resided in me all along. The knowing I have stored like a memory wanting to come out of me. This memory is the truth. I was scared when all of this opened, and not knowing what was happening to me did not make it any easier.

I trusted as I learned about the spirit world and about other concepts relating to things most people do not even have an understanding of. To leave it all behind and surrender to the ultimate finding and trusting within.

Bringing it finally to myself a higher feeling of peace, calmness, quietness, bliss and love.

Acknowledgements

❁

Su, your many calls, and our late night around the clock talks will always be remembered and cherished. Your love, kindness and understanding when all this started with me will always hold a special place of gratitude in my eyes.

Debbie, thank you for the support and being such a strong help in the beginning steps of the unknown. Our talks and time together will always be valued and respected.

Bill, our connection helped me believe. I trusted as the power of your words kept me going. Thank you, for honoring all the times we needed to meet. The phone calls and your words will never be forgotten as they pulled me through my transformation.

Angela, how do I put into words all the gratitude felt for someone that kept my life alive? I will hold the love in my heart for all the hours you spent taking care of me. Your gentleness and patience towards all that you had to witness will always be blessed by my heart. Thank you for keeping him alive…

John, sometimes the realm of reality does not always make sense. At times the understanding still holds much unexplained reasons. The times we shared together pulled out the deepest and most hidden elements of who we are. Every moment will be sacred to me. Thank you for all the love, laughter, tears, and reassurance. The heart will always know.

Editing, I thank all of you for being considerate of the time line, honoring and not questioning my guidance. The love from you to help me edit and pull this together will forever float in the waves of unseen love. Thank you and the love and blessings will always be sent from me to you. I am grateful that the ones who knew the story could share in this experience with me.

Su, heartfelt love sent to you for all the long hours and hard work editing. Thank you for going back to the remembrance of all the experiences we shared. I will always hold them dear in my heart.

Terri, message of love caught and captured within a few words of this thank you... Your patience and peace to take the long hours you spent with out sleep will always be remembered from me with compassion and gratitude.

Eric, abundance of tranquility and warm thoughts for all your understanding and hard work put into this. Thank you for having so much faith in me and for all the talks of support.

Toni, the speck of time unfolds with flourishes of kindness for taking the time to help and be a part of this. Thank you for listening and being a part of this journey.

Jane, the circle of recycling with compassion shared will always recycle back with how grateful I am to you. Thank you for the late and up all night hours spent to structure the beauty and flow of this story. Your design of the cover can truly be seen and felt with all the love and compassion you have for the illusion of my story with him. Beautiful.

Sandra, Thank you for taking me in and treating me like your own daughter. You and Su have been the only ones on this journey since the very beginning. You mean the world to me. I am grateful for all the talks you helped me through.

Lizabeth, thank you for helping with the key note, and making sense of so many things for me. You are such a caring and amazing person. I enjoyed are time together, and the talks that got us through.

Libby, much love for making me smile, while we spent time editing until the sun came up. Thank you for showing me the way to cleanse and get my body in shape. I thank you and Scooter for such a loving environment. I am so grateful I was in such an amazing energy and loving space to final this story.

So many others have been a part of my journey that have not been added to this story. The other stories will come into existence and be acknowledged for all the love and care given. Thank you to all the friends that acknowledged and supported "Who, I am."

I am grateful I listened to my guidance learning all I did through them. I have so much respect for the other realm, the elders, guides and all the entities.

To reach the author;
truessenceofhope@gmail.com

CPSIA information can be obtained
at www.ICGtesting.com
Printed in the USA
FSOW01n1656070218
44294FS